Smoke, Cle...
Red Hot ...
And You'd Have The World's
Most Effective Aphrodisiac.

He stood, stretched and massaged his temples. Quickly, before she could blurt out anything embarrassing, she turned and folded down the covers. Kicking her shoes aside, she climbed into bed and pulled the covers up around her ears. If she pretended to be asleep when he came back, she might be able to stay out of trouble.

His shirt was off before he closed the bathroom door behind him, revealing a tanned, wedge-shaped back with a few intriguing scars, which she did her best to ignore. Yawning, she closed her eyes and tried to focus on recreating the story of *Gretchen's Ghost* from the first line.

It was a lost cause. The picture that emerged on her mental screen resembled an X-rated video— one that left her feeling flushed and restless....

Dear Reader,

Get your new year off to a sizzling start by reading six passionate, powerful and provocative new love stories from Silhouette Desire!

Don't miss the exciting launch of DYNASTIES: THE BARONES, the new 12-book continuity series about feuding Italian-American families caught in a web of danger, deceit and desire. Meet Nicholas, the eldest son of Boston's powerful Barone clan, and Gail, the down-to-earth nanny who wins his heart, in *The Playboy & Plain Jane* (#1483) by *USA TODAY* bestselling author Leanne Banks.

In *Beckett's Convenient Bride* (#1484), the final story in Dixie Browning's BECKETT'S FORTUNE miniseries, a detective offers the protection of his home—and loses his heart— to a waitress whose own home is torched after she witnesses a murder. And in *The Sheikh's Bidding* (#1485) by Kristi Gold, an Arabian prince pays dearly to win back his ex-lover and their son.

Reader favorite Sara Orwig completes her STALLION PASS miniseries with *The Rancher, the Baby & the Nanny* (#1486), featuring a daredevil cowboy and the shy miss he hires to care for his baby niece. In *Quade: The Irresistible One* (#1487) by Bronwyn Jameson, sparks fly when two lawyers exchange more than arguments. And great news for all you fans of Harlequin Historicals author Charlene Sands—she's now writing contemporary romances, as well, and debuts in Desire with *The Heart of a Cowboy* (#1488), a reunion romance that puts an ex-rodeo star at close quarters on a ranch with the pregnant widow he's loved silently for years.

Ring in this new year with all six brand-new love stories from Silhouette Desire....

Enjoy!

Joan Marlow Golan

Joan Marlow Golan
Senior Editor, Silhouette Desire

Please address questions and book requests to:
Silhouette Reader Service
U.S.: 3010 Walden Ave., P.O. Box 1325, Buffalo, NY 14269
Canadian: P.O. Box 609, Fort Erie, Ont. L2A 5X3

Beckett's Convenient Bride

DIXIE BROWNING

Published by Silhouette Books
America's Publisher of Contemporary Romance

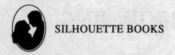

SILHOUETTE BOOKS

ISBN 0-373-76484-7

BECKETT'S CONVENIENT BRIDE

Visit Silhouette at www.eHarlequin.com

Printed in U.S.A.

DIXIE BROWNING

is an award-winning painter and writer, mother and grandmother. Her father was a big-league baseball player, her grandfather a sea captain. In addition to her nearly eighty contemporary romances, Dixie and her sister, Mary Williams, have written more than a dozen historical romances under the name Bronwyn Williams. Contact Dixie at www.dixiebrowning.com, or at P.O. Box 1389, Buxton, NC 27920.

One

Leaning forward, Carson Beckett removed the weights from his ankles and flopped back onto the exercise mat, exhausted and depressed. It was taking too long to regain his strength this time. And hell, he was still in his prime. Chronologically, at least. He knew of guys who reached retirement without ever having suffered so much as a hangnail. Not many, but a few. At the rate he was going, about all he'd be fit for was dusting a desk chair with the seat of his pants.

The occasional patch-up job was to be expected; he was a cop, after all. But a concussion, a black eye, a total of eleven broken bones counting arms, legs, fingers and ribs, all within the space of less than three years? That was pushing it.

At this rate he might even reconsider taking up that offer of a teaching post at the university. According to Margaret, the woman he was planning to marry as soon as he was up and running again, a degree in criminology was wasted on a policeman.

Carson poured himself a glass of water. Tap water, not the other stuff. Better the enemy you know, as he always told Margaret, who was never without her bottle of designer water. "Do you know where that water's been?" he would tease.

Nine times out of ten she would frown and glance at the label. The lady had a lot going for her—looks, talent, ambition—but her sense of humor was notoriously deficient.

All the same, Car told himself as he stretched and flexed his lean six-foot-two body, it was time to toe up to the marriage mark. Neither of them was getting any younger. Margaret was a year and a half older than he was, but looked five years younger. She'd made it plain that children were not an option, as she had her career to consider, but then, his mother would be happy enough to see them married. She would go on hoping for a grandchild as long as she was capable of hoping for anything, but after awhile...

In the bathroom that had been added on after he'd bought the old shotgun-style house outside Charleston, Carson peeled off his sodden sweats and stepped under the shower, flinching as he adjusted the head for nail-driver pressure. Nothing like a hard stream of cold water pounding down on his scalp to jump-start the brain.

It was several minutes before he realized that not all the pounding was water. Someone was at his front door.

Wrapping a towel around his waist, he barefooted it down the hallway and opened the door a crack, expecting the pizza he'd ordered earlier. He'd been practically living on the stuff for weeks.

"Hey, man, I was about to give up on you. Got a message from the chief.'' The voice was hoarse, the face familiar.

Shivering as the rain-laden March wind streaked past him into the house, Carson stepped back and let his friend and partner inside. "You look like hell, Mac."

"Look who's talking," the younger man croaked.

"Come on in, there's still some coffee in the pot." The two men had joined the force the same year and had worked together on numerous cases, sharing too much stress and bad coffee.

The stocky, redheaded policeman flung the rain off his hat and ducked inside. He opened his mouth to speak and sneezed instead. "Jesus, Car, I'm sorry."

"Bless you. Sounds like you need something stronger than coffee."

"Can't. On duty." Mac McGinty dragged forth a soggy handkerchief and blew his red nose. "What I came for, Chief says you might as well stay out another week." Carson had been out for the past three weeks on disability. "Everybody's got this flu thing, or whatever it is. Miserable stuff. Makes you feel like you been kicked all over."

The cop looked down at the fresh scars visible under the towel on his buddy's bare legs, and swore. "Yeah, well…like I'm saying, you come back now, you'll be laid up another month."

"Didn't you take your shot last fall?"

"You know me and needles. I figured if all the rest of you guys got shots, there wouldn't be nobody for me to catch it from."

Carson shook his head. "Tell me something, man—how'd you ever pass the physical? When they X-rayed your skull, didn't it register empty?"

"Yeah, yeah, yeah, so I sneezed on you. All I've got

is a cold. It's those other jokers you got to watch out for. I mean, Eddie, he's been out since last Thursday, running a fever, coughing his head off.'' The redheaded policeman forked back his hair, replaced his hat and reached for the door.

"Sounds like I'm needed."

"No way. Some of the first guys to go down are already starting to come back. Chief says your immunity system's probably compromised or something."

"Or something," Carson Beckett said dryly, watching his friend dash out to the unmarked car.

Glancing at the relentlessly gray skies, he shut the door and turned toward the kitchen to see if he had any canned chicken soup on hand. Just in case. The pizza, when and if it was delivered, would do for breakfast.

As guilty as he might feel about being out on disability for so long, the chief was probably right. Whatever bug was going around, Carson couldn't afford to risk it. He didn't know about his immune system, but tangling with a drug dealer armed with a two-ton truck, followed a few months later by having his unmarked car creamed by a kid riding a chemical high was about all he could handle at one time. He was beginning to feel like that old Li'l Abner character—the guy with his own personal black cloud hanging over his head.

He missed work. Missed the boredom of routine calls and paperwork, the adrenaline rush of closing in on a tough case, and most of all, missed the camaraderie of guys he'd worked with for years, even those he didn't particularly like.

It was his life, dammit. It was what he did—who he was.

He found a can of chicken noodle soup, opened it and dumped it into a pan. Adding garlic salt and black pepper, he debated his options. He could report in tomorrow and catch up on some of the paperwork that was part of being a cop these days.

Or he could use the rest of his downtime constructively. He had some pressing personal business he'd put off for too long, starting with Margaret.

It had always been more or less understood in both families—hers had lived next door for at least a generation—that unless something better came along for either of them, they would end up together. The Becketts were big on family. Strong ties, deep roots. Margaret was his mother's goddaughter, and Kate, his mother, was increasingly fragile, in the early stages of Alzheimer's. Both he and Margaret had agreed that they owed it to her to marry while she could still be a part of the festivities.

Carson had a habit that had developed into a policy over the years. On any to-do list of more than three items, he always tried to shorten the list by first tackling the one that could be finished the quickest.

Which meant that before he got caught up in wedding prep—in his family, marriage was a big deal—he needed to fulfill a promise he'd made to his grandfather before he died. A promise to clear up a generations-old debt owed by the Becketts to a family named Chandler.

Ever since a cowboy from Oklahoma named Chandler had handed over an undisclosed sum of money to an earlier Beckett, asked him to invest it, and then disappeared, the debt had gone unpaid. The Becketts had thrived. No one knew what had happened to the original Chandler, but a bundle of stock had been handed down through the Beckett family, with each subsequent generation intending to track down the Chandler heirs to make restitution.

Three days, tops, and the deed would be done. One more item he could mark off his list. Next would come formally popping the question and keeping his mother supplied with bridal magazines, fresh photo albums and blunt-tipped scissors. She was totally focused on weddings.

Barefooted, dressed in jeans and an open flannel shirt, Carson ate the soup from the pan. Table manners had been instilled in him from the time he was allowed to eat in the dining room with the family, but as a bachelor living alone, he allowed himself a certain amount of leeway.

He would have to clean up his act—one more thing on his to-do list—but not yet. It could wait until he was back on duty. Meanwhile, he would plan on one day to drive up to Nags Head, a day to locate the address and hand over the money, and another day to get back home. He could have made it in two days, but unless he got out and walked around every couple of hours, his knee and God knows what else would freeze up on him.

But the deed would be done. Finally. Unfortunately, the stock was now worthless, as the Becketts were inclined to procrastinate. The only record of the original debt was word-of-mouth, and PawPaw, who might have remembered hearing a few details from his own father, had died in January at age one hundred and two after suffering a series of strokes. For various reasons, neither of his sons was able to take on the task, and so it had been left to Carson and his cousin, Lance Beckett.

It was Lance who had come up with the idea of hiring a genealogist to track down the Chandler descendants. They'd shared the cost and each agreed to chip in ten grand of their own, intending to locate the heirs, hand over the money and mark the debt paid in full. It might not be enough; on the other hand, it might be a terrific return on what could easily have been the loan of fifty bucks, if you didn't figure in compound interest. Back in the late 1800s when the debt had initially been incurred, fifty bucks might have been considered respectable money.

Lance had already fulfilled his part of the promise by tracking down one of the two heirs and repaying his portion of the debt. He'd gone further than that—he'd married the woman.

Now it was Carson's turn. Unlike Lance's heiress, who had moved east from Texas, Carson's heiress had originated in Virginia, daughter of a high profile trial lawyer named Christopher Dixon and one Elizabeth Chandler Dixon, both deceased; granddaughter of a retired judge known as old Cast Iron Dixon and a wealthy socialite with the unusual name of Flavia. Both maternal grandparents deceased.

The Chandlers were thinning out, it seemed.

"Well, thank the Lord for small mercies," Kit Dixon muttered under her breath, screwing the cap back on her India Ink drawing pen. The two jerks who'd been arguing so loudly on the other side of the church had evidently decided to make peace—or at least to move their argument to more appropriate surroundings.

One of the reasons she liked this old cemetery so much was the peacefulness. It was little more than a wooded knoll in a sea of marsh grass, home only to countless birds and small animals.

Kit hated anger, hated arguments. Always had. Even after all these years, loud, angry voices still made her stomach ache.

As quiet once again descended over the surroundings, she leaned against a mossy tombstone and gazed out over the cypress trees, the wind-twisted scrub oaks and a cluster of cedars. Chalky white marble gravestones of all shapes and sizes stood out against the dark foliage. Small ones with lambs on top—tall ones with angels. The lambs were her favorites.

It was perfect. She could easily visualize ghosts rising like smoke from the ancient graves. Now that the last sketch was done, she was ready to bring her watercolors. Atmosphere was far more important than getting a perfect drawing. During that fleeting time before nightfall she could sweep in the values and the muted colors—fifteen or twenty minutes for each illustration, and she'd be finished. After that she'd give the manuscript one last polish, hand it over to be typed, and *Gretchen's Ghost* would be finished. It wasn't even due at her publisher until the first of April.

Brushing the leaves and dried grass from her seat, Kit paused to touch a leaning marker, worn far too smooth to read. "Who are you?" she wondered aloud. "If I knew your name, I'd use it in my next story."

She often used names she found on tombstones or on mailboxes, mixing first names and last. It gave her a sense of being connected to the past. And although she hated to admit it, she desperately needed to feel connected to someone—to something solid. She wondered sometimes if everyone felt that way, especially as they grew older.

But then, most people she knew had someone, somewhere.

Kit had someone. She had her paternal grandparents. She would probably even put in an appearance at their fiftieth anniversary party. She made a habit of dropping in unannounced every few months, partly out of a sense of duty, but mostly because it irritated her grandfather so. She would stay for half an hour and then leave. Leaving was the best part of all, because she could.

And because she knew it drove her grandfather wild. It wasn't his granddaughter he wanted, it was what she represented—the last link with his only son. And she ought to feel sorry for him, she really should, only she couldn't. She knew him too well.

So maybe she'd skip the party and get herself a dog.

Maybe she'd get a dog and take it to the party.

Or maybe she'd invite Keefer, the surf-bum she'd shared a house with last summer. It would serve him right. Her grandfather, not Keefer, who wouldn't have been impressed if she'd told him she was a royal princess. Three things impressed Keefer. Good grass, big surf and big bazongas.

Kit didn't have big bazongas. She practically didn't have any at all, not that it mattered. An author-illustrator of two published children's books with another one almost finished, her first book, *Claire the Loon,* had been optioned for television. When she'd first been notified, she hadn't believed it. When it had sunk in, she'd walked three feet off the ground for a week.

Of course nothing had come of it so far. Odds were, nothing ever would. She'd been told by her agent not to get her hopes up, as far more books were optioned than ever made the final cut, so other than treating herself to a mammogram, an eye exam and half a gallon of Tin Roof Sundae ice cream, she hadn't spent a penny of the option advance. It was in the bank earning a pathetic rate of interest.

Her real bread and butter, not to mention her rent and her art supplies, came from waiting tables. It was the perfect job. In season, the tips were easily enough to live on, yet the hours allowed her plenty of time to write. As there were usually job openings all up and down the Outer Banks in season, she was able to pick up and move as often as she liked if she needed a fresh locale.

That was just one more thing her grandparents disapproved of. No permanent address. They called her lifestyle immature, among several less flattering things. Perhaps it was. More likely it was her own brand of claustrophobia. Whatever it was called, she had a deep-seated need to prove her independence, and for the last seven years she'd been doing just that.

Not the way her mother had, with alcohol and lovers. Her grandparents never failed to remind her of her mother's twin weaknesses at every opportunity. Both, Kit was convinced, were a result of being married to a man who had all the warmth of an empty igloo. The irony was that Kit had just enough of her father in her—not his cruelty, but his steely determination—to defy her grandparents and build a life for herself. And although she felt justly proud of her small publishing accomplishments, there was no room in her pragmatic, hardworking, self-supporting lifestyle for artistic temperament.

Okay, so she enjoyed being able to dress any old way she pleased. So she liked old cemeteries. After working eight hours a day in a noisy restaurant, with clattering cutlery and people constantly making demands, she found old burial grounds restful.

Besides, it came under the heading of research. Both her published books had been ghost stories, involving pirates and shipwrecked sailors as well as children and animals. It was her thing. Her bag, as Keefer would say. Start with a quirky animal personality, throw in a large helping of local history and a dash of fantasy, and voilà. *Gretchen's Ghost* was going to be her best yet.

After repacking her backpack, checking to see that she'd left nothing behind, Kit headed for the parking lot on the other side of the church. She had just reached the old wrought-iron gate when the stillness was rent by the sound of a single gunshot.

Startled, she froze and waited. A hunter? In March? At this time of evening? Wasn't that illegal?

Besides, who would hunt in a place like this?

When she heard the sound of someone speeding away she let out the breath she'd been holding. That's what it had been—an engine backfiring. That funny whining sound it had made when it was racing off probably meant it needed tuning.

Admittedly, one of the occupational hazards of being a writer of fiction, especially fiction that edged over into fantasy, was that a single backfire could instantly become a pirate landing or an invasion from another planet.

The church was used only for summer revival meetings, but the security light was still in service. Now the pink glow shone down on the graveled parking lot, empty except for Ladybug, her orange-and-black, hand-detailed VW. So much for the invasion from Mars, she thought ruefully as she dodged a patch of weeds.

She was nearly halfway to her car when she spotted what appeared to be either a shadow or an even larger clump of weeds.

Not a shadow. There was nothing nearby to cast such an oddly shaped shadow. And not weeds, either, it was too solid.

A trash bag? A big, injured dog? A deer?

Oh, no—someone had shot a deer!

Maybe the poor thing wasn't dead—maybe the Fish and Wildlife people could...

After the first few steps she froze. Then, sick with dread, she crept closer. "Omigod, omigod, no, please," she whispered, backing away.

It was an old man, and he was obviously dead. There was a black hole in the middle of his forehead and a dark trickle of something that looked like blood trailing down his cheek from his left nostril.

Kit's snack of almonds and dried apricots threatened to turn on her. She swallowed hard and muttered, ''Gotta get help, gotta get help!''

But where...? Who? Murder didn't happen in a place like Gilbert's Point, it just didn't.

But it had. And suddenly she realized that whoever had done it had to have seen her car. There couldn't be more than one like it in the entire county—maybe in the entire world.

She stared at the vanity plate she'd bought with part of her first advance: KITSKIDS. If anyone wanted to find her...

Edging around the still form lying on the weedy, badly graveled parking lot, she hurried to her car. Throwing her pack onto the other seat, she locked the doors, keyed the ignition and ground the starter.

Don't panic.

Cell phone. Why the devil hadn't she bought herself one of the pesky things and learned how to use it. Everyone knew how to use a cell phone.

Everyone but Kit.

But even if she'd had a phone, she didn't know the sheriff's number. Wasn't there some automatic gizmo you could punch to get help in an emergency?

One of the reasons she didn't own a cell phone or a computer or any of the other gadgets everyone else in the world took for granted was that she was no good with gadgets.

''Nine-one-one, you ninny!'' Any child knew how to dial nine-one-one. Don't panic, don't panic.

She would go home and dial nine-one-one and tell whoever answered that there was a dead man out at the old church on Cypress Mill Road. And they would ask her name, and she would have to go in and testify, and her grandfather...

Oh, shoot.

There was no one in sight when she raced up the steps and slammed inside the unpainted frame house she'd rented only a few months ago. Slinging her backpack toward the table, she grabbed the phone and started dialing, hardly remembering to breathe.

Answer, answer, answer the blasted phone!

Someone answered. A woman who sounded as if she resented being disturbed. "There's a dead man in the cemetery—no, I mean in the church parking lot out on Cypress Mill Road!"

"Name, please?"

"Name! I don't know his name! I just told you, he's dead! Someone shot him! Oh—" Cold sweat beading her forehead, Kit slammed down the receiver. She took several deep breaths, her hand still on the receiver. All right, she'd done her duty. She had reported the crime; it was out of her hands.

Name. The woman had wanted her name, of course. "Idiot," she muttered, feeling the horror of it all over again.

Should she call back and give her name? But if she did that, she might have to go in and answer all sorts of questions, and the story would get in the papers and old Cast Iron would be after her again to come to her senses, and she didn't feel like brawling with him right now, she really didn't.

On the other hand...

All right, Katherine, for once in your life, think logically.

Had she done everything she could?

Absolutely. She had reported the crime. Knowing her name wouldn't help anyone solve it.

Was she in any personal danger?

How could she be? She'd only done her duty as a citizen.

On the other hand, her car had been the only one in the parking lot. It was certainly easy enough to identify, even without the vanity plate. For all the killer knew, she could have witnessed the whole thing instead of only hearing it.

Maybe she should go stay with her grandparents until the murderer was caught. She could even go on with her job, for that matter. Regardless of how often she moved she was never more than forty-five minutes or an hour away, depending on season and time of day.

There was probably some murky psychological reason why she'd untied the apron strings, but never quite cut them entirely, but she didn't need to delve into that now. Taking a deep, steadying breath, Kit weighed her options. She could disappear. All she had to do was pack up and move again. But that would leave her boss in the lurch, and it would mean starting a whole new set of illustrations for *Gretchen* somewhere else.

She could go back to Nags Head. She knew the area, knew where the best jobs were, and where she could probably find an affordable room this early in the season, maybe even her old one.

Taking another deep breath—at this rate, she'd be hyperventilating—Kit glanced despairingly around at the shabby old house she had rented semi-furnished. It was just beginning to feel like home. She had even named the raccoons that regularly raided her garbage can.

Face it, Katherine—the gypsy life is losing its appeal.

Reluctantly, she dragged out her suitcase and the banana boxes she used for packing her painting equipment, copies of her books and all the messy details of her profession. The legal pads, which she bought by the score; the bulging files of correspondence and another file, pitifully thin, of royalty statements.

Could she be exaggerating the risk? The gunman was probably a hundred miles away by now. Why on earth would he come back to the scene of the crime, knowing he might have been seen?

All right, so she was thinking logically. That didn't mean the killer thought logically.

On the other hand, she really liked Gilbert's Point. It was much quieter than Nags Head, which was a circus during the peak season. She liked the people here. She had a decent job that allowed her plenty of free time for her real career. Not all employers were as understanding, but Jeff Matlock at Jeff's Crab House was proud of her. Even though he was a bachelor, he'd bought copies of both her books.

Besides, her rent was paid through the end of March. And unlike the beach area, Jeff's season was just getting started. The snowbirds—the semiannual flight of yachtsmen fleeing the snow and ice via the inland waterway, and returning in the spring once the north began to thaw—were beginning to migrate.

Kit stood at the door of her closet, staring at the eclectic mixture of grunge clothes—her tie-dyes and hand-embroidered jeans that her grandparents so despised—and the few decent dresses she'd kept for emergencies. Weddings, funerals, autographings and anniversary parties. Somewhat to her disgust she'd discovered that she was too much her father's daughter to dress inappropriately for public occasions.

With a sigh of resignation, she closed the closet door. She would stay, but she would definitely be on her guard.

If nothing showed up in the paper tomorrow indicating that the murderer had been caught, she would call the sheriff and offer to come in for questioning. Not that there was anything else she could tell anyone. She'd heard voices, she'd heard a shot, she'd seen a body.

And she'd run away.

Two

"Are you sure she's not here?" Carson asked the white-haired kid with the mahogany tan. He'd arrived at Nags Head just before dark the day before and spent a miserable night in a hotel, wondering if he was coming down with whatever bug Mac McGinty had been generous enough to share with him.

"Kit? Man, she's long gone. Got a Christmas card from some place called Gilbert's Point."

"You got any idea where it is?"

"Across the bridge, I think."

"Which bridge?" According to the map, the place was full of bridges.

"Hey, dude, geography's not my gig, y'know? Sorry. She was a cool roomie, too, but I mean, it happens, y'know?"

Dude knew. He was a cop, after all. When it came to education, a degree in criminology was nothing compared to thirteen years on a big-city police force. Ignoring the view through the open door of a coffee table made of beer cans and layered with dirty clothing, and the smell of pot and old pizza, Carson was tempted to forget the whole thing. He'd woken up feeling like leftover hell, but as long as he'd come this far, he might as well see this business through.

Dude? he thought, his footsteps gritting on sandy broken concrete on his way to the car. Was that retro, or had it never quite gone away? At the advanced age of thirty-seven, he was beginning to notice a few recycled trends.

Obviously Kit Dixon's lifestyle was nothing at all like that of her cousin Liza. Not that it mattered. He didn't have to approve of the woman, he had only to find her and hand over the money and the bundle of worthless stock certificates, in case she was into collecting useless antiquities. Some people collected "collectibles," which could cover almost anything.

It was nearly noon when, with the help of aspirin and his GPS unit, Carson reached Gilbert's Point, which consisted of a few old frame houses, several shabby restaurants, a crab processing plant and a dozen or so boats tied up at the plank wharf. Squinting against the harsh sunlight reflected off the inland waterway, he surveyed the scene, wondering where to start.

Or even *whether* to start.

He could always bundle up the stock certificates and the cashier's check for ten grand and address it to Katherine Dixon, in care of general delivery, Gilbert's Point, North Carolina. The post office would do the rest. If they even had a post office.

Not a chance. The Becketts' buck-passing days were over. Besides, the job was already half done—he was here. With just a slight additional effort, he could wind things up. Case closed, only a hundred years late.

But the three days he'd allowed himself were getting used up in a hurry. At this rate he'd be lucky to get back home by the weekend. It would help if he didn't feel so lousy. Hot, cold and sweaty at the same time, with a head that was threatening to self-destruct.

It occurred to him that some real food might help. Not that he was particularly hungry, but the combination of too much coffee, too much greasy fast food on the road and too little sleep didn't help what else ailed him. Besides, at a local restaurant he could probably kill a couple of birds with a single stone.

He struck pay dirt at the first place he stopped. After ordering hot clam chowder and a fresh tuna sandwich at a waterside restaurant called Jeff's Crab House, he popped the question.

"You happen to know a woman named Katherine Dixon?"

Instead of answering, the waitress called over the owner, a tall, loose-limbed type with a handlebar moustache, who took his time crossing the empty room that was just now being set up for lunch. "Jeff, this guy wants to know where to find Kit."

Jeff looked him over before replying. "You a friend of hers?"

Carson stretched a point. "Friend of the family. I was in the area and thought I'd look her up."

Another minute passed. Carson appreciated what the other guy was doing—sizing him up. Under other circumstances, they could have swapped credentials, IDs—hell, the whole bag of tricks, but his head was throbbing, his throat was getting rawer by the minute and every bone in his body ached.

"You want to hang around, she'll be working the five-to-nine shift," the proprietor finally said, "I don't reckon she'd want me giving out her whereabouts. Probably not home yet anyhow."

He was tempted to flash his badge, but that might give the wrong impression. He didn't want to get the woman in trouble, he just damned well wanted to find her so he could go home and go to bed for the foreseeable future.

And anyway, in a place this size, he could knock on every door in less time than it took to search through the phone book.

"Okay. Uh...like I said, our families are connected." In a manner of speaking, he added silently. "We've never actually met, though, so would you mind telling me what she looks like, in case I run across her?"

Jeff frowned. He fingered his handlebar mustache. "Guess it wouldn't hurt none. 'Bout yea high." He held a hand up to his shoulder. Five-six, Carson interpreted. "Lots of hair, kind of brown with some red in it. Gray eyes, freckles. She's a real nice lady and a hard worker." The guy was on a roll, so Carson let him talk. "Smart woman. Good-looking, too. She walks most everywhere, but you might see her car around. Hard to miss it. Old VW Beetle painted orange with black spots on it. Did the paint job herself," he added admiringly. "I had me one, same year, back when I was in high school."

Carson had learned a long time ago that a lot more information could be gained by allowing a witness to ramble on at his own pace than by asking specific questions. He'd take it all in and sift through it later when his head wasn't threatening to explode. Right now, he needed coffee, food and another handful of aspirin.

Having evidently decided that Carson wasn't a threat to anyone, the proprietor shifted his weight onto the other foot, apparently settling in for a lengthy visit. "I tried to talk her into selling it, but she said it was like family. Even gave it a name. Ladybug. Got one o' them what-chacall vanity plates on the stern. Kitskids. Writes kids' books, but she don't have no kids of her own, not s'far as I ever heard of. Hey, Bambi, Kit ever mention any family to you?"

From across the room, the pretty waitress with black acrylic nails shook her head. "Less you count all the strays she collects. Kit feeds any critter that don't bite back."

By the time Bambi brought over a steaming bowl of Hatteras-style chowder and a tuna sandwich thick enough to choke a mule, Carson had lost his appetite. What had seemed a short-term deal on his to-do list was turning out to be a real headache. Literally.

"This guy said to give you this." Bambi held out the scrap of paper. "Certified hunk. If you're not interested, how 'bout I try my luck?"

Kit had come in early to ask Jeff how to find the sheriff's office. It was probably located in the county seat, wherever that was. She could have called and gotten directions, but having made up her mind to do her duty as a citizen, she needed to show up in person and get the whole thing over with before she lost her courage.

"Here? You mean someone came to the restaurant looking for me?" It took a moment for the impact to sink in. "Did he—did he say what he wanted?"

The redhead shrugged. "You, I guess. Said he was a friend of the family. He asked a whole bunch of questions about where you lived and when you were coming in. Jeff told him you'd be in at the regular time. Hey, you okay? You didn't eat none of that crab salad last night, did you?

Jeff told you it was for the critters. He made it up a couple of days ago, and crab don't keep."

Ignoring the question, Kit asked anxiously, "You didn't tell him where I live, did you?" Not that he couldn't find her easily enough. There weren't that many houses in Gilbert's Point.

"What, me tell a stranger something like that? No way, hon." She snapped her chewing gum. "Good-looking, though, if you like the type."

Kit didn't ask what type. She really, really didn't want to know. The thought that someone could find her so easily was scary enough. The old church was several miles from Gilbert's Point. Maybe she shouldn't have panicked, but after more than two hours, her heart still hadn't settled down. If she'd done the right thing and gone in instead of just calling nine-one-one, the sheriff could have done his job by now and she wouldn't be jumping at shadows.

On the other hand, if she turned herself in now and offered to tell everything she'd heard—which wasn't all that much, really—the sheriff would want to know why she hadn't come forth immediately. Then she would have to tell him her name and it would get in the papers and her grandparents would see it, because Chesapeake was just over the state line in Virginia and everyone in the area read the same papers and listened to the same news stations.

And then her grandparents would demand that she come live with them, with all that implied, and she couldn't, she just couldn't. If and when she mended that particular fence, it would be because she wanted to, not because they demanded it. She owed it to her mother's memory not to get sucked down that particular drain.

Meanwhile she was going to have to stop reading romantic suspense. Her imagination was active enough, without adding fuel to the fire.

By the time he left Jeff's Crab House, Carson knew he wasn't going to finish the job that day. His headache had backed off to a dull throb, but his eyes burned, his throat felt raw and every muscle in his body ached. The bones that had been broken ached twice as much. All he wanted at this moment was to crawl into bed and sleep for a year, but if there was a hotel in the immediate vicinity, he'd missed it.

He sneezed, grabbed his head to keep it from flying off his shoulders, and muttered, "Thanks for sharing, McGinty."

He was on his way out the single road leading to Gilbert's Point when he saw the little orange VW barreling after him. Black spots. Sort of like a ladybug on steroids. Shoving his personal problems into the background, Carson wondered if the lady could be following him. Had he let slip the fact that he intended to hand over ten grand while he was asking questions?

He didn't think so, but then, he wasn't operating at peak efficiency.

There couldn't be more than one black-speckled orange VW in a place this size. Slowing, he looked for somewhere to pull over. The Landing Road was little more than an old cart trail that had been brought up to minimum standards with a few loads of marl and oyster shell, with drainage ditches on both sides. No place to pull over— barely enough room to pass.

Five minutes. He'd give her the spiel and hand over the goods. Then he could go somewhere and die with a clear conscience. The way she was kicking up dust, she was evidently eager to catch up with him before he got away.

He slowed, stopped and pulled on the parking brake. They were near the intersection of Landing and Waterlily Roads, but so far as he could see, theirs were the only two cars on the road. This shouldn't take long, Carson promised himself.

Good thing, too, he added. He'd just run flat-out of juice.

Opening the door, he got out, steadied himself for a moment, and waited until she came to a halt a few feet from his rear bumper. Then, levering himself away from the support of his dark green SUV, he headed her way.

His legs were shaky. Maybe he should have eaten his lunch, but by the time he'd been served, food hadn't seemed all that great an idea.

He was within ten feet of the hand-painted VW when he saw her roll up her window. She locked her door, then leaned over and locked the passenger door.

Well, hell. What now? Find the nearest hollow tree, leave the goods there, then write and tell her where to find it? If she wrote kids' books, she might be into kids' games.

Tough. She'd picked the wrong player this time.

He was still trying to figure out an approach when she rolled her window down an inch and shouted for him to move his car, then rolled the window up again.

Move his car? Had he missed something? It occurred to him that she might not have gotten the message that he was looking for her. In that case, maybe she wasn't trying to catch up with him, but just wanted to pass. Thought he was a tourist, maybe, watching a flyover of cormorants.

Okay, so what now? Try to reason with her through a

layer of steel and glass? Put yourself in the lady's place, Beckett. She's alone, she finds herself being accosted by a strange man. Reason enough to be spooked, right? The world was no longer a safe place, if it ever had been. Who knew that better than a cop?

The women of his family knew better than to stop if ever a stranger tried to flag them down. They'd been taught to lock all doors and pass the buck by calling the highway patrol. In this case, he was the next best thing, only she had no way of knowing it.

Feet spread apart to keep him from reeling, Carson held up both hands, palms out, in the universal sign of peace. "Hey, I'm one of the good guys, lady."

Cautiously, she inched her window down and peered at him suspiciously. From where he was standing—aside from the eyeball assault of color: orange car, red hair, purple dress or whatever she was wearing—she appeared to be a damned fine-looking woman.

Irritated as hell, but a looker.

Make that angry, he corrected a moment later when she lowered the glass another two inches.

Make that scared. In fact, terrified would not be an overstatement.

Well, hell. What now? This wasn't in the script. Under any other circumstances he'd have walked off and let her go unreparated, or whatever the proper term was. His whole body ached like a boil. He was running on fumes. And dammit, he hadn't come all this way to leave the job unfinished.

Taking two steps forward, he said, "Look, for both our sakes, let's get this over fast, all right?"

Slowly, he reached inside his buckskin jacket, planning to hold out his badge to reassure her.

"Noo-o-o!" she screamed. "Just get out of my way!"

Wrong move. He held out his hands again as if to prove he was totally harmless. Evidently the message failed to get through. She gunned the engine. The Beetle jerked forward. Carson tried to leap out of the way, but his reconstructed knee wasn't up to the job. It buckled, and before he could catch himself, he went down, his head in a tangle of weeds bordering a blackwater ditch.

She backed up and slammed on the brakes. She was out of her car in an instant, wild auburn hair flying around her face, purple shirt flapping around long legs covered in a pair of tie-dyed tights.

She was wielding a tire-iron in a way that was anything but reassuring. "Open your eyes," she demanded in a quavering voice.

No way, lady. I'm safer playing dead.

She crept closer. He squeezed his eyes shut, hoping she'd be convinced and leave him alone. Nothing in the genealogist's chart had indicated a strain of insanity in the Chandler genes, but then the lady genealogist hadn't gone into any personal detail.

"You're not dead. I saw your eyelids twitch. I hardly even touched you."

She hadn't touched him at all, but only because he'd jumped out of the way just in time. She hesitated, but he could hear her breathing. She was still looming over him with that damned tire iron. The right tool in the wrong hands could be lethal.

"Darn you, open your eyes!" she whispered fiercely. By then she was so close he could feel the heat of her body, feel her breath brushing his face. "I barely touched you, you can't be dead," she declared.

He was having trouble regulating his breathing. It would be just his luck to have a sneezing spell. He felt her knees press against his side, felt the soft pressure of cool fingertips on his throat, then on his chest.

Yeah, I'm alive, he was tempted to tell her. Keep on touching me like that and I'll show you just how lively I can be, headache or no.

Fat chance. He was fighting on too many fronts to take on one more. She smelled like...cinnamon? Apples?

Something equally innocuous...and equally tempting.

She touched his forehead and jerked her hand away. He wanted her fingers back. They were cool, soothing, and God, he needed that. What the hell was he supposed to do now? None of this was in the script. If he opened his eyes or even so much as twitched a muscle, she'd probably cold cock him with that damned tire iron.

"You're alive, I know you are. I don't even see any blood, so you can't be seriously hurt. But while you're down I just want you to know that I didn't see anything, not one blessed thing, so you don't have to worry about me. Just because my car happened to be in the parking lot, that doesn't mean I saw what you did. I was on the other side of the cemetery. I couldn't even hear what you were fighting about."

Breathing through clenched teeth, Carson mentally assessed the damage. He was winded, but probably in no worse shape than before. Unless he slid into the ditch and drowned. If she didn't stop pressing her knees into his side, that was a distinct possibility.

What the hell was she talking about? A cemetery? Fighting? She sure as hell had seen him.

"Well," she said tentatively. "I probably shouldn't leave you here in case another car comes. Besides, you're blocking the intersection."

Tentatively, she picked up his hand and tugged. He felt something tickling his cheek and hoped it wasn't alive, because the last thing he needed on top of everything else was an infestation of chiggers.

"Look, I know you're not unconscious, I can tell by the way you breathe."

He could have told her that his breathing would be a lot more convincing if she weren't so close…and so damned *female*. Were pheromones considered hormones? His were supposed to be out on sick leave.

He could sense her studying him as if he were something under a microscope. Thank God he wasn't armed. Sometimes he carried when he was off duty, but not when he was this far out of his jurisdiction. Besides, this wasn't that kind of a case. Hadn't started out that way, at least. But who knows, with a crazy woman…

"I didn't hit you that hard. I didn't even feel a bump," she said defensively.

He didn't know what to say, and so he said nothing. If his head weren't hanging lower than his feet, he'd have been content to stay right where he was for the foreseeable future.

On the other hand, with a crazy woman feeling him up…

Get your hands off my body, lady, that's private property you're invading.

Her hair hung down and tickled his face. She was muttering under her breath, something about a gun. What the devil was she talking about? She didn't even know he was a cop—they'd never got that far in the introductions.

Kit was looking for his pistol. He had to be wearing one, because why else would he be wearing a leather coat on a day like this? As long as you stayed out of the wind, it felt almost summer.

Had he had it in his hand when she'd hit him? If so, it

could be anywhere, even in the ditch—although she hadn't heard a splash.

The murder weapon. Oh, my blessed mercy!

She had to find it before he came to and hold it on him until she could get help. Yell for one of the men on the wharf to call the sheriff.

Being able to hand over his gun as evidence would make up for not giving her name when she called, but first she had to find it. One side of his coat was caught underneath his body, and so she started, carefully patting him down. His body was hot. Hot, hard and...

Squatting beside him, she leaned over and slipped her fingers under the other side of his coat. Right-handed men wore their guns on the left side, didn't they? And vice versa?

She had no way of knowing which handed he was. Some men shoved their guns into the back of their belt, but he was lying on his back and he was too heavy for her to roll over.

And then her fingers touched something that felt like leather. Too flat to be a gun or a holster...

Frowning, she managed to ease it out of an inside pocket. "A badge?"

"Satisfied?" His voice sounded like iron grating on concrete.

She gasped and dropped the badge, scrambling backward and trying to look as if she hadn't been caught with her hands in places they had no business being. "Look, whoever you are, we're going to have to move you, else you'll slide into the ditch and drown, but don't try any funny business, because we're being watched." She had no idea whether or not the men working on the waterfront a few thousand feet away were paying any attention, much less whether they could actually see what was going on. "So don't think you can get away with anything."

"Wouldn't think of it," he rasped. His eyes were still closed. She didn't know whether to trust him or not.

"Can you move?" She leaned forward on her knees again and studied his face, which was hardly reassuring, but then at this point it would take the Daughters of the American Revolution and the Mormon Tabernacle Choir to reassure her.

"Can you open your eyes?"

No way, lady. As long as he didn't open his eyes, Carson told himself, he could pretend this was all a bad dream. All of it...the purple banshee, the smell of cinnamon and apples, the babbling testimony—those cool hands pawing over his body.

Don't try any funny business? What was she, a comic book character? There was nothing even faintly funny about any of the past forty-eight hours.

He groaned, and the woman caught her breath.

Man, I don't need this complication, Carson thought tiredly. She clutched his hand and gave a few experimental tugs. If he had a lick of sense he'd have crawled on his knees, climbed back in his car and hightailed it out of here the minute he realized she was criminally insane.

If I had a grain of sense, Kit thought, I'd have left him where he fell and got hold of the sheriff, and let him send for an ambulance. And while she was at it, she could have mentioned that they might want to bring along handcuffs, because the man sprawled out beside the road was probably a murderer, never mind that he had a badge inside his jacket.

Or she could call nine-one-one again, report a man down at the intersection of Landing and Waterlily Roads and then drive up to Chesapeake. Her grandparents might not approve of her, but they wouldn't want anything awful to happen to her.

Oh, it would make the papers, all right. The churchyard murderer hit by a car driven by the only witness to the crime.

On the other hand, if she left him here, he might lose consciousness and slide down the ditch bank and drown.

"What am I going to do about you?" she whispered. "I'm tempted to—"

He opened his eyes then, and Kit found herself staring down into the bluest eyes she had ever seen. More cobalt than cerulean, she thought fleetingly, but darker now with what could be pain.

"Are you…all right?" she asked hesitantly. Merciful saints, the man was on a mission to shut her up permanently, and she was worried about his health?

She studied him carefully. His eyes were closed again. He was breathing heavily, as if he were in pain. She didn't know if he'd lost consciousness or not, but she needed another look at that badge, and this might be her last chance. The thing could have come from a toy store, for all she knew. Probably had.

But not his gun. There was nothing wrong with her ears; toy guns didn't make the same sound as what she'd heard in the churchyard.

Her hand moved toward his jacket. He opened his eyes, focusing on her face, not the hand that hovered over the flap of his coat.

"It's real," he said as if he'd read her mind. With a smile that looked as if it hurt and disappeared almost instantly, he said, "I'm a few miles out of my territory, but—" He covered his mouth, sneezed, and then groaned.

"Bless you," Kit murmured automatically. "What are

you—that is, are you looking for someone in particular?''
Like me, for instance? She added silently.

If he was from the sheriff's department, he'd probably
traced her through one of those gizmos people hooked
onto their phones. Nine-one-one probably had it for people like her; people who didn't want to get involved.

Well, crud. No matter how tempting it was, she
couldn't leave the man lying there. Any minute now a car
could come peeling in off Waterlily and crash into his car
or run over his legs. Probably cream Ladybug in the process. There wasn't much room for maneuvering.

"Look, I'll help you get up and into your car, but I
really don't know anything more than what I told you over
the phone. Told your dispatcher, at least. I heard voices—
I couldn't even tell what they were arguing about. Then
I heard a shot, only I thought it was a backfire, and
then—''

There was barely room, but she managed to position
herself behind him. Reaching down, she hooked her arms
under his. Lordy, what a waste, she thought before she
could stop herself. He was a big man. A big, beautifully
constructed man, she couldn't help but notice. With un-
combed black hair that was overdue for a trim, a lean,
pale face that hadn't recently seen a razor, he wore west-
ern boots, jeans that were worn in all the right places, a
black shirt and a buckskin jacket that looked as if it had
been through a few battles.

Get your mind on what you're doing, you ditz!

"I'm going to sit you up," she said, bracing to use
herself as a counterweight. "Help me out here, you weigh
a ton."

"Give me a minute, okay? I'm just winded."

"More than that, if you ask me. Well, you didn't, but
I'll get you back inside your car, anyway. The rest is up

to you. If you're a real policeman, you can call one of your deputies or something. If you're not—well, like I said, I didn't see anything. Honestly.''

By the time they managed to get him on his feet again, Kit had touched him in places she hadn't touched any man in years. Her palms tingled from the heat of his body. If it turned out he really was a sheriff or a policeman, she would simply repeat what she'd said over the phone—which wasn't all that much, come to think of it. But this time she would answer any questions he asked to the best of her ability. Then, if he insisted on taking her in to make a statement, she could do that, too, because no crook was going to come near her as long as she was under police protection.

At least, that was the way it worked in suspense novels.

Except when the cop turned out to be the villain.

Well, she wouldn't think about that. Besides, this one looked more like a hero. Not that he was classically handsome by any means. He had one of those crinkly mouths that looked as if he smiled a lot when he hadn't just been run off the road. That aggressive jaw that was badly in need of a shave, and a pair of dark eyebrows arched perfectly over beautiful blue eyes. On a woman, she might have suspected tinted contacts, but this man, whoever he was, was too rugged. He looked as if he didn't give a hoot what anyone thought of his looks.

Correction: at the moment, he looked as if he were about to collapse.

''Are you hurting anywhere in particular?'' she asked cautiously. The last thing she needed was a lawsuit. That would be all her grandfather needed to reel her back into the family fold.

He inhaled deeply, shook his head and winced. ''Nowhere in particular. My grandmother would have called it feeling all-overish.''

She didn't want to hear about his family, she had enough problems with her own. She glanced at her car and then at his larger SUV. "Can you drive? That is, maybe I could drive you home and then come back for my car.''

"Long walk," he rasped. She'd been right about his mouth. It crinkled into a quick grin that melted the last of her resistance. If he was one of the bad guys, she could easily outrun him. She doubted if he'd shoot her right in plain sight of the wharf and any passerby.

"Well, maybe I could follow you to make sure you get home safely. I mean, if you really are a policeman, I guess it would be all right.''

"Ms. Dixon?"

Astonished, she said, "You know my name?"

"Katherine Chandler Dixon?"

"Who *are* you?" She edged away. "Did my grandfather send you?"

"No, mine did," he said, and then bent double in a fit of coughing that made her throat hurt just to hear it.

"You're sick," she said flatly. "There's a hospital in Elizabeth City and one on the beach. I think there are some other medical facilities, too. Take your pick.''

Recovering, he shook his head. Under the dark shadow of beard, his face looked the color of raw plaster. "Don't need a hospital. On my way to recovering from a few busted bones, I picked up a bug. It's no big deal—mostly headache. I just need to sleep it off.''

"Look, if you'll tell me where you live, I'll see that you get there, one way or another, all right? The rest is up to you.''

"Charleston," he said with another of those twisty

grins. If she didn't know better, she'd think he was deliberately trying to disarm her.

"Where's that?" And then her eyes widened. "You mean the one in South Carolina?"

"Yep. Last time I saw it, it was." He appeared to be breathing easier now that the coughing fit had passed.

"I'm certainly not going to drive you to Charleston, but if you're staying somewhere around here, I'll help you get there."

"Nags Head last night. Checked out this morning." He named a hotel about three mileposts from where she'd worked last summer.

Shaking her head slowly, Kit made up her mind. Lord, if she ever wrote an autobiography, no one would believe it. Not that anyone would be interested.

"You're coming home with me," she said firmly. Lord knows she'd taken home scruffier-looking creatures. Four-legged ones. Besides, her home was within shouting distance of practically everyone in the village. "It's not much, but at least you can rest up until you feel like telling me what this is all about." The man knew her name. She wanted to know what else he knew about her. "You can rest on the couch until you're feeling better. It opens up and I can let you have a spare pillow."

Carson wanted to refuse. Hell, he wanted to be back in Charleston in his own bed, with the telephone off the hook and a solid week to do nothing but sleep.

At the moment, though, if she'd offered him a doormat, he would gratefully have accepted. "Need to talk anyway," he said. He could rest up for a few minutes, speak his piece, hand over the goods and by that time he'd be good to go.

Good enough, at any rate.

"You wait here," she said. "I'll move my car off the

road—nobody'll bother it. I can drive a stick shift, you don't have to worry about that.''

He shook his head, winced and said, ''Automatic.''

''Whatever. I just don't want you on my conscience. You're in no shape to drive and my car will be all right here. There's no crime around these parts.''

Hearing her own words, Kit wondered just when she had stepped through the looking glass. How about murder? And no matter how peaceful it might look on the surface, Gilbert's Point saw it's share of drug traffic, not to mention the occasional Saturday night celebration that got out of hand. So far as she knew, the Coast Guard took care of the drug runners and a night in jail took care of the boozers. But murder—that was scary.

''Give me the keys,'' she growled. ''I'll help you in and—''

He helped himself in, moving as if he'd been stretched on a rack, but moving under his own steam. That was encouraging.

''You can take a nap if you want to, I don't have to be at work until five and it's only four-twenty. Are you allergic to aspirin? How about chicken soup? Jeff at the Crab House makes really good chicken soup.''

She could hear her mother now. ''Katherine, do you have to drag home every stray creature in the world? I'm not running a zoo, you know,'' she would say. At least, she would when she was sober enough. Or when she was home. Perhaps if she'd been home more often, or sober more often, Kit wouldn't have adopted every stray she saw, from homeless cats to tailless lizards to broken-wing birds.

It had never worked out, anyway. Her father had seen to that. He made her watch once while he stuffed a litter of abandoned kittens into a sack and drowned them in the Chesapeake Bay.

And then she'd had to serve her term in the closet for defying his orders. It was usually only a matter of a few hours, but once, after one of her strays had infested the house with fleas and they'd had to get the exterminator in, she'd been locked in the closet for twelve hours straight. She had cried herself sick, then she'd begun making up stories.

She probably had her father to thank for her career.

"Hot tea's supposed to be good for colds, too. And onions. Not together, of course, but..."

Carson let her babble. All he wanted to do was lie down and close his eyes. He never got sick, *never*. Been busted up a time or two, but he'd never caught any of the bugs going around. Until now.

By the time she stopped the car in front of a house that was about the same vintage as his own, it was all he could do to slide out of the car. His overnight bag was in the back, but he lacked the motivation to reach for it.

Passing by an assortment of bowls and pans on the front porch, she opened the door and pointed toward the back of the house. "Bathroom's back there, last door on the left. Couch is through there, help yourself. I'll put the kettle on and call to see if today's chicken soup's ready. Jeff makes it fresh every day."

Her voice had a soothing quality, which was surprising coming from a woman who was at worst a dangerous psychotic, at best, a compassionate flake. "There's an afghan on the back of the couch. When you're feverish, you probably don't need to be chilled. Or is it the other way around?"

She left, muttering something about starve-a-cold, feed-a-fever, but by that time Carson was down and nearly out.

A moment later he could sense her presence, even though his eyes were closed. Don't talk any more, he wanted to say, it hurts my head.

"I won't talk any more, you probably just want to sleep. Why don't I go get my car now, and I'll stop by the restaurant and bring you some chicken soup before I go to work."

He felt a drift of something light and wooly over his body. She hadn't tried to remove his coat, but she tugged at one of his boots briefly before giving up. He could have told her that there was a knack to pulling off boots, and she didn't have it. At that point, he didn't care.

Bye-bye, angel. Wake me up in a few weeks, all right?

Three

This is the right thing to do, Kit thought in an effort to reassure herself. After running the man down, she could hardly walk off and leave him there. He was injured, possibly even ill. It was only natural to be uneasy—any normal person would be uneasy.

All right, so she was more than uneasy, she was scared stiff. But she was still functioning, and under the circumstances that was pretty cool.

With shaking fingers, she dialed the Crab House. "Look, Jeff—I might be a few minutes late coming on shift, but I'm going to stop by first, and could you please have a quart of chicken soup ready to go?" She listened, darting quick glances toward the living room. "Uh-huh—that's right, he found me."

Someone had been asking questions about her? And she'd been fool enough to drag him home with her.

Maybe her grandfather was right—she was a clear case of arrested development.

But the man had known her full name. That had brought her up short, and before she could come to her senses curiosity had outweighed fear, and now she was stuck with him.

Fortunately, he was out like a light, as she simply wasn't up to the job of dragging him out and dumping him beside the road.

Raking her hair from her forehead, she thrust her car keys in her pocket and hurried down the path, wondering if she'd left enough room for Ladybug. Without thinking, she'd parked the Yukon in the place she usually parked her own car. Second thoughts, and third ones, dogged her steps as she hurried along the road. How could she have walked out and left a strange man asleep in her house at a time like this?

Even under normal circumstances Kit never invited men to sleep in her house. Sleeping over implied involvement, and Kit had a whole series of rules concerning getting involved with a man, starting with No Way and ending with Just Say No.

Growing up in a family that was everything proper on the outside and totally dysfunctional behind closed doors had left scars that she was still trying to heal—or if not to heal, at least to hide.

In other words, she mocked silently, you're a chip off the old block.

Early on, it hadn't been quite so evident that once her father left for his office, the whole house seemed to breathe a sigh of relief. Back then, her mother would wait until just before dinner to take the first drink. During the day they would go places, just the two of them. Movies, museums, shopping...to the zoo. On rainy days they might play Fish or cut paper dolls from old fashion magazines. She'd loved that, making up stories about each one.

For Kit's eighth birthday her mother had given her a bride doll. In later years Kit always connected the doll in her mind with a large, gold-framed wedding picture that had hung in her mother's sitting room. The bride in the picture wore a full-skirted lace gown and pearl-seeded veil, her eyes aglow in a classically beautiful face. Standing beside her, but not touching her stood the groom, Christopher Dixon, looking handsome and chillingly uninvolved. That was before her mother's drinking spiraled out of control.

Oh, they'd been a pair, all right. According to her grandfather, Betty Chandler had set out to trap herself a rich husband, and in a weak moment, the judge's only son had allowed himself to be caught.

So far as Kit knew, her father had never had a weak moment in his entire life. If the judge was known as Cast Iron, then her father, a junior partner in a prestigious law firm at the time of his death, could surely have been called Stainless Steel.

Three days after her parents' funeral—they'd died in a plane crash when she was eighteen—she had started making plans to move. They had lived only a few miles from the elder Dixons' spacious white brick house on the Chesapeake Bay. Her grandparents were more than capable of dealing with the estate. Not that they would have welcomed her input even if she'd dared offer it.

Poor Grandmother—the judge insisted on the formal titles—had been crushed by the death of her only child, but under her husband's cold, disapproving eye she had quickly rallied. By the day of the funeral she'd been her old self to all outward appearances, which was all that mattered to the Dixons. Cool, polite and properly withdrawn.

The next day her grandfather had sent for Kit to discuss her father's will. Instead of obeying the summons, she had gone back upstairs to her room and started packing, boxing up her collection of books, her paints, her clothes and her mother's wedding photograph. Then she'd locked the front door and headed south with one hundred and thirty-seven dollars and no prospects.

And she'd done just fine. Missed a few meals along the way and spent more than a few nights in her car, but she'd learned quickly and been lucky. Before her grandfather could enlist every law enforcement officer in the Commonwealth of Virginia to track her down, she'd called to let them know she was all right. She hadn't told them where she was, but since then she'd continued to call and occasionally drop in for a brief visit.

She honestly didn't know why she bothered, since all they did was criticize and try to coerce her into returning to the fold. Her grandmother's gentle chiding was as bad as her grandfather's harsh disapproval. According to the judge, Kit was just like her mother—weak, flighty and immoral. Just look at the way she dressed, for one thing—which, of course, had made her dress all the more outrageously. And working as a waitress? No member of his family had ever worked in a menial position.

She was a darned good waitress. She'd like to see him try and keep up with orders and unruly patrons without losing his cool on a busy night at the height of the tourist season.

Still, they were all the family she had. Deep down, she probably loved them. At least, she couldn't bring herself to cut them off completely. One of these days they might even need her, and if that time ever came she would be there for them. But she would never go back and allow them to treat her the way they had treated her mother.

Thinking always made Kit walk faster. She was halfway along Landing Road when she glanced up to see someone trying to open her car door.

Her steps faltered. Had she locked it?

Of course she'd locked it—although as a rule she didn't bother. Gil's Point was hardly a haven for car thieves.

"Hey, you!" she shouted.

The man glanced over his shoulder. Several men down at the boat dock looked up. Gil's Point was that kind of place—no more than a mile or so from one end to the other, surrounded by tidal marsh on three sides, the canal on the other. One of the things she liked best about it was the neighborly feeling among the dozen or so families, who were mostly kin and had lived there forever.

"That's my car," she yelled, her red sneakers pounding on the hard-packed marl. If it was in the way—and it was—she would move it. She didn't need any stranger doing it for her. Ladybug had a ticklish transmission. For ticklish, read desperately ill.

"Hey, Kit, you all right?" one of the fishermen hollered.

The man who'd been nosing around her car looked from her to the fishermen and back again. Without a word, he turned and loped over to a red pickup truck with one blue fender that was parked off to one side on Waterlily Road. Climbing in, he slammed the door shut and roared off in the direction of 158.

For several moments Kit stood and stared after him, puzzled, but not wholly alarmed. Maybe he thought she'd run out of gas. Maybe he was only trying to be helpful. But then why had he run away?

And why had the sound of his truck struck a nerve?

Almost everyone around here drove trucks, and one sounded pretty much like another, at least to her undiscriminating ears.

Suddenly a chill coursed through her, like a cloud shadow racing across the marsh grass. It wasn't panic, she told herself. Panic had been when she'd found that body with a bullet hole in the forehead. Since then she hadn't had time to panic.

Well...she might have come close a time or two.

But it was broad daylight. No one with half a brain would try to steal a car in front of the whole town at a quarter of five in the afternoon. It was probably just someone who collected vintage VWs. She'd had several offers. Seeing it parked on the roadside, he might have thought it was for sale and was checking it over to see if he was interested. Maybe he'd been looking for a For Sale sign.

But then, why run away?

Because he'd recognized the Ladybug from the church parking lot and was looking for a way to silence a potential witness? Because he'd been looking for identification so that he could find out where she lived, sneak into her house late at night and smother her in her bed?

"The curse of the writer's mind," Kit muttered. She could create drama from three ants in a sugar bowl.

On the other hand, there had been a murder—she hadn't imagined that. Fisting her hands in frustration, she wailed in the direction the truck had disappeared, "Blast you, I didn't *see* anything!"

A startled mockingbird flew from a nearby bay tree, and she expelled her breath in a frustrated sigh. What now? Hyper imagination or not, she knew better than to touch her car without having someone check it over first. She'd seen the news. She read hard-edged suspense novels. He could have tampered with her brakes or at-

tached one of those thingees to the ignition that would
make it explode as soon as she turned the key. Or maybe
even when she opened the door.

God, what a day—and she never swore. Never!

She felt like crying, only she never cried, either, so
what now? Unlock the door and risk getting herself blown
up, or wait and let someone else take the risk?

Well, that wasn't much of an alternative.

Maybe her policeman would know what to do. That is,
if he really were a policeman. A policeman, she reminded
herself, who knew not only her full name, but knew how
to find her. Not even her grandparents knew where she
lived. At least, she didn't think they did.

No, it had nothing to do with her grandparents. It was
just a little too coincidental, the way he'd turned up knowing her full name on the same day she'd heard a shot and
discovered a body.

The trouble with being a fan of suspense novels was
that it opened your mind to all sorts of possibilities.

The trouble with being a writer of children's books was
that you didn't have a clue as to how to act on those
suspicions.

Turning back toward the village, Kit forced herself to
examine the situation logically. She could never remember which side of the brain controlled which function, but
her logical mind—a legacy, no doubt, from a long line of
legal types—was actually every bit as good as her creative
mind.

Item one: she had witnessed a murder.

Well, she hadn't—not really. At least she hadn't seen
who had done it. Not that it mattered if the murderer
thought she could identify him.

Item two: she had called to report the crime. Hadn't
answered any questions—hadn't even waited to be asked,

but at least she'd reported it. It was up to the sheriff to do the rest.

Item three: there was a strange man asleep on her couch, one who might or might not be who he claimed. One who probably had no connection to what had happened this morning. The key word was *probably*. He'd told her his name was Beckett on the drive to her place, and he'd known her full name and known where to find her, even though she had moved three times in the past two years.

And she'd been gullible enough to invite him into her home?

So much for a functioning brain. Putting out leftover food for the local wildlife was one thing; taking a stranger home with her and giving him a place to sleep was something else. Obviously she'd inherited her judgment from her mother's side of the family.

Think, Katherine, think! Could there possibly be some connection between her Virginia grandparents and a policeman from South Carolina? The badge might or might not have been real. She had only Beckett's word, from their conversation in the car, on who he was and where he was from. She wasn't even sure that was his real name.

It was just the sneaky, underhanded sort of thing her grandfather would do, sending in a Trojan horse. With the elder Dixons, control was always the issue. In her case, it was control of the money she stood to inherit. They'd briefly lost control of their son when he'd married someone outside their social circle. They hadn't been able to control their daughter-in-law any more than they could control their granddaughter. That had to gall a man who could control a jury with the lift of a bushy eyebrow.

Kit could have told them why, of course. In both cases, the money simply wasn't enough. Her mother had lacked the courage to leave a hollow situation, but not Kit. She might be lacking in judgment, but she had courage.

When she had visited her grandparents, she'd been almost amused to discover that she had her own control issues. The last few times she'd been there her grandfather had made a point of promoting his protégé, a lawyer named Elliott Saddler. Kit had met him a few times before she'd left home—he was a member of the same firm where her father had been a partner.

She hadn't been fooled, not for a single minute. Not that Elliott was anything like the judge, but Kit knew how her grandfather's mind worked. She was twenty-five years old. Legally there was no way he could pull her strings, but if she were to marry someone like Elliott, who thought the judge walked on water, the old despot would have her right where he wanted her. Right where he kept his wife and where he'd tried to keep his daughter-in-law: under his cast-iron thumb.

Kit glanced at her watch as she stepped up onto the old wooden wharf and hurried to the restaurant on the far end. Twelve minutes to go before she was supposed to report for work. "Jeff, is the soup ready? I've got a houseguest, and he really needs an infusion of your chicken soup. I think he has the flu or something."

The tall restaurateur grinned, and then frowned, looking her over. "You don't look so good. Don't you come down with nothin', y'hear?" He handed over a quart jar in a brown paper bag. "I'm counting on you for the breakfast shift startin' next week. We're getting more layovers every day."

Kit and Bambi regularly traded shifts, which enabled Kit to use mornings for scouting out locations and working on her drawing, evenings for writing and finishing up her watercolors. The tips at the Crab House were nowhere near as good as the ones at the beach, but living was cheaper, she liked the place, liked the people and the flexible schedule suited her fine.

It had been the scheduling that had prompted her to move away from Nags Head once the season had ended last year. The work was grueling and by the time she finished her shift, there was never any energy left for her real occupation.

"See you in a few minutes. I'll pay you then," she called over her shoulder.

Trotting along the wharf with the jar of soup clutched to her bosom, she greeted the few fishermen mopping down their boats and readying their equipment for the next day.

"You got car trouble?" one of them asked.

She shook her head. "I went to bring Ladybug back home, but forgot my keys." It was a lie—not even a plausible lie, but she wasn't about to explain.

The young fisherman grinned and shook his head as if to say, *Just like a woman.*

Kit jumped off the end of the wharf onto a well-worn path that wound its way past several ancient live oaks, a deserted house nestled in an overgrown yard and a cedar grove before reaching her unpainted rental. It had once been painted white, and the gingerbread trim was still mostly intact. One of these days she might use it as a location for a haunted-house story.

The soup was piping hot. Kit knew in advance that Jeff wasn't going to want to take her money. She had a feeling that with the least bit of encouragement, he would try moving their relationship to another level, but it wasn't going to happen. He was one of the nicest men she knew, but Kit wasn't up for anything even hinting at romance.

The late afternoon sun had already turned her tall windows to stained glass by the time she reached her front porch. As worried as she was about her car, she decided to let her guest sleep as long as he wanted to, leaving a note to let him know where to find the soup and a pot to heat it. If he was gone when she got back from work, so much the better.

If he was still here, then he'd better be ready to answer a few questions, she thought grimly, changing into her work uniform of white jeans and a Crab House T-shirt. She braided her hair neatly—or as neatly as possible, considering that her hair had a mind of its own.

On the way out she glanced in at her stranger.

Mercy, he was something. Kit didn't tempt easy—in fact, she could have sworn she was immune to temptation of the masculine variety. But this man was something else, with those incredibly blue eyes, that thick black hair and the kind of body—lean in all the right places and muscular in all the rest—that could make a grown woman weak in the knees.

She didn't need another event in her day, she really, really didn't. Uneventful suited her just fine.

Four

It was dark when Carson awoke. His first thought was that his back was broken. His second thought was that he needed to locate the men's room. But then he took in his surroundings and it all came rushing back. After stops in Manteo and Nags Head, he'd ended up at one of those waterway stopovers that was so small it wasn't even on the charts, chasing an elusive woman with an obvious homicidal bent. A woman who drove an orange car painted to resemble an insect and who spoke in some code known only to the initiated. A woman with the face of a homemade angel, who might be missing a few gray cells up under that mass of curly auburn hair.

He sat up and rolled his shoulders experimentally, taking stock of his surroundings. Using the eerie glow of a security light down on the waterfront that came in through the windows, he located a lamp and switched it on. Then, after flexing his bad knee experimentally, he stood and took a couple of test steps.

So far, so good. A few of his hinges might need oiling, but he was able to function. At least his head was no longer being attacked by a swarm of tiny demons armed with pickaxes. A smart man would find the john, leave the money and get the hell out.

Okay, so he wasn't too smart. He intended to hang around long enough to make sure all the loose ends were tied up before he left, because this was it, as far as he was concerned. Debt cancelled.

He limped carefully toward the room at the end of the hallway, half expecting his hostess to pop out from behind one of the closed doors. Had she said something about going to work? He couldn't remember.

Eying the claw-footed, iron-stained bathtub, he thought wistfully of a long, hot soak, accompanied by a couple of fingers of Jack Daniel's, with maybe a Don Williams CD in the background, or a pre-season ballgame on WSB radio.

Uh-uh, better not risk it, he told himself. It would take a block and tackle to get him out of the tub once the whiskey and hot water went to work on him.

Besides, the lady might misread his intentions.

After splashing his face and washing his hands with her scented soap, he felt slightly more human. Then, catching his reflection in the mirror, he grimaced. No wonder she'd been spooked. The face that stared back at him was not particularly reassuring.

On the other hand, he wasn't running for office. He was a cop. At the moment he wasn't even that, he was merely a guy on a personal mission, acting as an emissary from past generations of Becketts. Once he'd accomplished his goal he'd be on his way home, stiff knee and all, ready to tackle his second objective.

Marrying Margaret.

Funny thing, though—now that he thought about it, he didn't recall feeling this reluctant a few days ago when he'd decided to put off setting a date until he'd wound up this reparations business for PawPaw.

Must be the flu bug. It sure as hell wasn't the love bug that had bitten him. To be perfectly honest—and at the moment, his brain wasn't up to being anything else—the last thing he felt like doing was tying himself down to a lifetime of city living, business entertaining, weekly golf and the occasional cruise.

Carson had his own ideas when it came to business entertainment. Beer and barbecue in the backyard with Mac and his wife and kids a couple of times a year suited him just fine. As for golf with his country club buddies, he didn't have any, didn't want any. His favorite sports were baseball and fishing, with NASCAR running a close third. As for any cruises he took, he would prefer a bass boat on Lake Moultrie.

On the other hand, his mother was counting down the days. Now and then she might lose count, but the gleam was still visible in her eyes whenever Margaret dropped in while he happened to be there. Kate—his mother— spent hours each day cutting pictures from bridal magazines, sticking them in an album and carefully decorating each page with hand-drawn orange blossoms. She still knew him most of the time, but the companion they'd hired for her had told the family that sooner or later she might need to be moved to a facility that specialized in Alzheimer's patients.

God, he felt like crying, just thinking about it. It had crept up so silently with no warning at all. The odd paranoia, the sudden lapses of memory, the pauses in the middle of a conversation when she would smile as if she'd lost her train of thought. Which, of course, was precisely what had happened. And was continuing to happen with more and more frequency.

Your mission, should you choose to accept it, he told himself mimicking the format of an old TV show called *Mission Impossible,* is to marry Margaret as quickly as possible, have hundreds of photographs taken and give your mother the task of arranging them all in one of her albums.

It might be the last thing he could do for her that would give her real pleasure. And he couldn't put it off much longer.

Sighing, Carson switched off the bathroom light and headed for the kitchen. The first thing he spotted was the note on the table, weighted down by a chunk of clam-shaped marl. Following his hostess's instructions, he located a pot and set about reheating the chicken soup he found in the refrigerator. Ten minutes later he was back on the couch, his feet on a newspaper on the scarred coffee table, a bowl of the best chicken soup he'd ever tasted on a tray in his lap. He'd match it against his Aunt Becky's cooking any day, and Rebecca Beckett, Lance's mother, had been winning awards for her cooking ever since she'd mixed up her first batch of oyster fritters.

Relaxing in the shabby, surprisingly comfortable living room, Carson wondered what Margaret would make of Kit's decorating skills. The blue Mason jar of Carolina jasmine was a nice touch, although half the blossoms had fallen off. He even liked the basket of dried weeds in the corner. The unframed pictures on the wall lent a whimsical touch, although he doubted if Martha Stewart, let alone Margaret's fancy decorator friend from New York, would approve of kid art thumbtacked to unpainted walls, minus so much as a mat.

Still, he kind of liked the place—maybe because he was feeling considerably better. Bare wooden walls, bare wooden floors. At least there were no clothes piled on top of beer-can tables like the Nags Head duplex.

His gaze moved back to the plank-and-cinderblock bookshelf. Evidently the lady was a reader. Suspense, nature guides, murder mysteries, art books and…

Children's books?

Hmm. Matlock at the seafood place hadn't mentioned any kids. But then, he'd been more interested in her car. Maybe she had a kid, and said kid was staying with Daddy, as Mommy obviously had a few problems to work out.

In his line of work he saw too many such cases. In most of them, there was no good answer. Usually, though, if a family functioned at all, it was better to leave a kid in the home than to remove him and turn him over to an overworked, understaffed system. Some kids didn't take to fostering. He'd seen bad results from either decision, including a few that just plain ripped his heart right out of his chest.

When it came to family relations, he'd been spoiled, and was smart enough to know it. There weren't many Becketts left, but the few that remained were close, getting together for holidays, birthdays and anniversaries. Lance and Liza would be adding to the roster most any time now.

It was those close family ties that kept him sane on his worst days as a cop. They also kept him humble, because he knew too well that not everyone was so fortunate.

At any rate, whether or not Ms. Chandler had any offspring, it shouldn't affect the reparations. His generation was repaying hers. Once it was done, if she wanted to pass it on, that was her decision. Ten grand wasn't much in today's world, but judging from the way she was living, it might provide a small cushion to fall back on. He might even suggest ways of investing it. PawPaw would have approved. He'd been a big-time investment banker in his day.

On the other hand, he thought, grimly amused, better not. This whole bizarre situation had started when a Chandler had handed over some money and asked a Beckett to invest it for him.

Carson finished the soup, considered seconds and decided there was no point in asking for trouble. Whatever bug Mac had handed off apparently affected different people in different ways. Headache, fever, congestion and muscular aches he could handle. Nausea was another thing altogether. As much as he loved fishing, if he'd ever been seasick a single time, he would have been a bank fisherman for the rest of his days. Lucky for him, he had an industrial grade stomach lining.

It occurred to him that this would be the perfect time to leave the cashier's check and the stock, and disappear. A receipt would have been nice, but a cashed check would be all the proof he needed if repayment ever became an issue.

So why not just do it and leave, Beckett?

The answer was a little too elusive for his foggy brain to wrestle with at the moment. For starters, the lady intrigued him, and he wasn't easily intrigued. She was a looker, if you liked wild hair, colorful, freewheeling clothes and earrings that looked more like fishing lures than jewelry.

Picturing Margaret's discreet silver studs and his mother's screw-back pearls that she called earbobs, he

shook his head. He knew very well his own family was
no gauge of today's fashions. The Beckett women were
typical of their social class maybe fifty years earlier.
Housedresses and straw hats for working in the flower
garden, flowered dresses and flowered hats for afternoon
affairs; dark crepe with pearls for more formal affairs. His
mama still wore white gloves and a hat to church, although some of the younger ladies of the congregation
wore slacks and none of them wore hats.

He tried and failed to imagine his mother's reaction to
Katherine Dixon. Fortunately, the two women would
never have occasion to meet.

Reheating the coffee that was left in the pot, he turned
over in his mind what he remembered of their initial contact. The woman had been ranting some wild gibberish
after she'd tried and nearly succeeded in running over
him. Something about not seeing something or other. And
cemeteries? *Gunshots?*

Whatever it was, it obviously held meaning for her.
She'd sounded frightened and angry, and so far as he
could recall, he'd done nothing to frighten or anger her.
Okay, so he'd approached her car—he hadn't come closer
than ten feet. Not close enough to cause her to feel threatened.

All evidence pointed to the lady's being a certified
flake. Granted, her looks and the gracefully awkward way
she moved, like a foal just getting the feel of his legs,
were enough to capture the attention of any man with a
viable hormone in his body, but once she opened her
mouth, all bets were off.

Yeah, so why didn't he stop thinking about her and get
on with what he'd come here for?

He rinsed his bowl and cup, poured the rest of the soup
back in the container and put it in the refrigerator, then

ran water in the pot. Dish-soaking was one of the first laborsaving devices he'd acquired after leaving the police academy, buying a house and setting up housekeeping. No self-respecting cop still lived with his parents, and he didn't like renting. Needed his own space, no matter how humble.

He was headed out to the car to bring in the briefcase containing the check and stock certificates when he caught sight of a figure jogging up the path, silhouetted against the pink security lights.

Too late, he thought, not even wondering why he wasn't more disappointed.

"Oh, good, you're awake! I was afraid you'd be gone—by the time—I got off from work," she panted. "I need to know—how can you tell if a car's been rigged to blow up? I mean, where do you look and what does a car bomb look like? Is it that plastic goop or does it have wires? I've read about it—well, you know—on shoes and things—but I don't know what it looks like."

Wacko. Batty as a cave.

She came to a halt a few feet away. He could smell the not-unpleasant essence of fried onions and something fruity and sweet. "Uh...you are a policeman, aren't you?" she asked hesitantly.

She was wearing red sneakers, a pair of plain white jeans, a T-shirt advertising Jeff's Crab House and a pair of earrings that would make any largemouth salivate. If there was a single flaw on that long, lean figure, it was well hidden. Her hair had been confined—more or less— in one long braid.

Carson found the total package fascinating, tempting and uncomfortably young. He felt ancient in comparison.

"Well? Are you?"

Am I what, dazzled? Oh, yeah. Tempted? Ditto. Sus-

ceptible? At any other time, and under any other circumstances—like a few years added onto your age and a few
subtracted from mine—that would definitely be an affir-
mative.

"Police detective Carson Beckett, at your service." He
thought he remembered introducing himself earlier, but
he might have forgotten. And hers probably wasn't a re-
tentive mind. "The soup was great, by the way. I left the
dishes to soak."

"Oh, good. Not the dishes, I mean—well, I'm glad you
liked the soup, but I mean about being a real policeman.
Did you say a detective? That's even better. Come on
back inside, this time of year it gets cool once the sun
goes down, and I don't think anyone will bother it for the
next few minutes." It was probably in the low sixties.
Cool was the last thing he felt.

But she wasn't through. "It's been there all this time—
I hated to leave it, but I didn't know what else to do.
Maybe there's nothing wrong with it. Sometimes I tend
to dramatize things."

That, he could believe. "You didn't think anyone
would bother what?"

"The Ladybug. Do you drink coffee at night? Do you
feel up to talking, or would you rather go back to bed?
Well, to couch, at least."

Carson had a feeling that a third party refereeing their
conversation would shake his head and walk off the field.
He knew *he* made perfect sense. She probably thought she
did, too, but they might as well be speaking two different
languages.

"I left it there at the intersection—my car, I mean.
Well, I had to get to work—there's only one of us working a shift since Jane left to get married. I was pretty sure
no one would bother it, but—"

She whirled around and plopped down onto one of the room's two chairs. "Oh, Lawdy, there's so much I don't know," she moaned, shucking off her sneakers to massage her bare toes.

Tell me about it, Carson thought wryly. "You want to start at the beginning?"

"Oh. That was this morning. You see, I do my sketches when I'm working the evening shifts, and then wait and add watercolor when I'm working mornings, because the light's just right. In the evening. For this book, I mean. All the illustrations for *Gretchen's Ghost* are set when the sun's just gone down and there are shadows, and—well, you're not interested in all that."

Interested? Carson was fascinated. Genuine oddities always captured his imagination, and he had yet to make sense of a single thing the woman had said—unless it was about the chicken soup. And she was speaking English.

"You see, it all started when I heard these two men arguing."

"Which two men?"

She flung out her hands. He'd noticed that about her, too—she used her hands when she talked, as if words alone couldn't convey the full message. "Well, if I knew that, then I could have told the sheriff and none of this would have happened. I mean, not the murder, of course—that had already happened, but my car. I need to know if it could be rigged to explode, only I haven't had time to find out. I couldn't leave Jeff without someone to cover for me, and like I said, Jane's married, and besides, the nearest garage is—"

Carson held up a hand. "Whoa. Back up."

She frowned. On her, a frown was roughly the equivalent of a megawatt smile on any other woman. He could almost see the wheels spinning. "My illustrations, you mean? Oh. You mean the murder."

And so she proceeded in her own unique style to relate the happenings of the past few hours. "See, first I heard these two men arguing, only I didn't see anything because I was on the other side of the church in the cemetery and there's this big grove of cedars, but then I heard this shot. I thought it was a backfire—at least I did at first when I heard someone drive away. I thought the engine backfired. It had a funny sound, like it might be groaning."

"The gunshot?"

"The engine. Sort of a zoom, zoom, and then a low whining noise like a jet plane flying really far away."

Right. Muffler pack. Carson listened without further interruption, having gradually concluded that at least a portion of what she said made sense when taken in context.

"Only when I got to the parking lot, there was my car and this—this dead body. So I came home and called the sheriff. At least I called nine-one-one and…well, that's about all, really. Except for seeing a man messing around my car."

He jumped on the simplest part of her statement. He did know she had a car—knew she'd left it out on the road. "You didn't retrieve your car yet?"

She shook her head. Now that she had decided to open up, she had that childlike expression of trust that gave him all sorts of misgivings.

"But it's locked and everybody here knows it belongs to me, so I was pretty sure no one would bother it."

Don't trust me, he wanted to say. Trust implied involvement, and involvement was something he didn't have time for. Under other circumstances he might have enjoyed indulging in a little meaningless sex—he'd been through a long dry spell where sex was concerned, and as reluctant as he was to admit it, there was something about the lady. As long as you didn't try to make sense of what she was saying.

After a night of inventive, uninhibited sex, he could hand over the check and walk away. Limp away. Crawl away.

Only you didn't do that to someone who trusted you. At least, Carson didn't.

Back to the issue at hand. "In other words, you can vouch for the locals. What about strangers?"

"We don't get many of those, not this time of year. Boat traffic, mostly, but people who tie up to refuel and eat at one of the restaurants don't go any farther than the waterfront. Not that there's that much more to see, just miles and miles of wetlands with a few wooded knolls. We don't even have a gift shop. Jeff sells T-shirts and souvenir mugs and things like that, but most people stop farther south where there are better facilities and more to see."

Carson had an idea that these small, hidden stops along the waterway served another purpose, but there was no point in bringing that up. Reluctantly, he gave up on the sex and set aside his reason for being there. It had waited a hundred years; it could wait another day. "Where's your phone book? First thing we need to do is make a few calls."

Rotary dial. Why wasn't he surprised? This whole place was an anachronism. While he waited for the call to go through, Kit paced. She'd told him to call her Kit. It suited her, he thought, watching as she moved around the room, pausing now and then to glance out the window. Foxy lady.

"Dad? How's Mom?" A long pause, and then, "Yeah, I found her." Another pause while his father asked if he was doing his exercises and had he known about the epidemic that had laid out half of Charleston's finest. He assured his father that he'd avoided that particular bug. And he had, for the most part, other than a few minor symptoms. His dad didn't need anything else to worry about.

"Look, I might be a day or so late getting home. How about calling the post office and—sure, that'll be fine. Thanks."

He hung up after accepting the usual parental admonishments. He was thirty-seven years old, for cripes sake. His mama was still calling to remind him of his dental checkup. At least she had been until she'd all but forgotten he was her son.

Oh boy.

Riffling through the phone book he found the number for the sheriff's office and dialed. Kit's wide, rainwater gray eyes watched his every move, full of curiosity and something else he put down to wariness. After identifying himself, he said, "About the body found out on—" He cocked an eyebrow toward Kit.

"Cypress Mill Road," she supplied.

"Cypress Mill Road," he repeated, "I'd like to come in and—" He frowned. "What d'you mean, what body? You didn't get a call about a murder victim earlier today?"

Kit moved closer, her breath feathering his neck. As much as he liked the attention, he needed to concentrate, and she wasn't helping.

"It wasn't a prank, dammit, it was a—"

Glaring at Kit, he listened while the jerk on the other end read him the riot act, the gist of it being that no body had been found, and manpower had been wasted checking out a prank phone call.

Kit grabbed his arm the instant he hung up the phone. "What?" she demanded.

"They say no body was found. Are you, uh, sure you saw something? You said yourself you thought it might have been a shadow."

Releasing his arm, she started pacing again, gesturing with her hands as if she were speaking aloud. He watched, fascinated, until she spun and glared at him as if he were somehow responsible for her predicament. "I know what shadows look like—they're a balance of alizarin crimson and thalo green."

He didn't say a word. The Martians had landed and his translator was AWOL.

"This was no blasted shadow, I'm telling you! That's what I thought at first, too, but it wasn't all that late, and besides, shadows don't have holes in their forehead. Shadows don't—" She shuddered. "Shadows don't bleed from the nose. Darn it, I know what I saw!"

"Right." God, Martian or not, he was tempted to hold her—forget the sex—he just wanted to hold her and tell her everything was going to be just fine, not to sweat it. Funny thing was, he was beginning to think she might really have seen something. Otherwise, why would she have called the sheriff in the first place? Whatever else she was, Kit Dixon struck him as the kind of woman who didn't like getting involved in anything rough.

Trouble was, she was already involved right up to her pretty pink ears. Something had happened, because she was obviously scared, and he'd lay odds she didn't scare easy.

Which meant that they were both involved. Temporarily involved, he stipulated silently. He could hardly hand over the check and take off, not until he was sure she'd be all right. Because he was a cop, sworn to protect and defend the innocent. Or maybe because he was a Beckett, and the men of his family believed in that old-fashioned thing called a code of honor.

Pain in the arse, is what it was. "So here's what we'll do then," he said, mentally laying out a plan as he spoke. "First thing tomorrow we'll check out your car—that is, if you're sure no one will bother it tonight." He wasn't about to go snooping around with a flashlight if there was the least possibility of a bomb.

Not that he thought there was—there hadn't been time. But if this turned out to be what he was beginning to suspect, it would pay to be cautious. Sooner or later the DEA would probably be involved, but it wasn't his call to make.

Her face was a shade or two paler than it had been a few minutes earlier. A handful of freckles stood out across her nose, making her look younger than he knew she was. According to the genealogist's chart she was twenty-five.

Too young for you to be thinking what you're thinking, good buddy.

He cleared his throat, which was still on the raw side. "When do you have to work tomorrow?"

"Same shift. Five to nine. I usually go in a few minutes early and stay after to set up for the morning trade."

"Good. First we'll check out your car and then we'll drive out to this church of yours and look around. After that, we might drop by the sheriff's office. And if you don't mind, I'll borrow your couch again tonight. Six a.m. suit you? It ought to be light enough by then, but a flashlight would come in handy."

She nodded, a dazed look on her peaked, not-really-pretty-but-beautiful face. "I feel like I'm on a runaway escalator. Sooner or later I'll either have to get off or crash. Trouble is, there's no getting-off place."

Carson wanted to touch her, to reassure her. He lifted a hand and let it drop. Don't go there, Beckett.

Hell, he was probably contagious, anyway. The last thing she needed was what ailed him.

The moment passed. "What do you eat for breakfast?" she asked.

"Cold pizza. Barring that, coffee and whatever."

"Yeah, well, it'll probably be whatever," she muttered as she shrugged and headed down the hall. "Turn off the light before you go to bed, okay? I don't like to waste electricity."

Five

Long after she had cleared the bathroom and closed her bedroom door, Carson lingered in the kitchen, washing the few dishes he'd left in the sink, which she had ignored. Then he rummaged around until he located a box of baking soda, mixed some in a glass of water, and used it to swallow a few more aspirin. His mama's favorite cure-all. Had something to do with the pH factor, not that Kate had ever put it in those terms, bless her sweet soul.

He wished to God it would help her now, but there wasn't enough aspirin and soda in the world to bring back a woman who was slipping a little farther away each day.

He yawned and went out to retrieve his overnight bag. He needed to get out of here, like yesterday. Yawning again a few minutes later, he switched out the lamp and reminded himself that this wasn't his case. He had more on his agenda than delivering a long overdue payment for a debt that wasn't even his own. But the lady needed a hand, and he happened to be on the scene. As a man, as a Beckett and as a cop, he owed her whatever assistance he could provide.

His body cried out for sleep, but his brain was still too wired to surrender, and so he lay awake thinking over the things she'd said, slotting them into the things he'd observed. Which wasn't a whole lot, in either case.

Still, whatever else she was, the woman was not quite the flake he'd first thought her. Taken in context, most of what she'd said even made sense. But what the devil was a woman like Katherine Dixon doing in a place like this, waiting tables at a restaurant that probably would see no more than a couple dozen customers on a good day? Maybe not even that many.

According to her, she'd had two books published, for cripes sake. Outside his mother's church circle and their fund-raising cookbook, he didn't know anyone else who had actually written a book and had it published. And this was no homemade job. Even he had recognized the name of the publisher.

He had offered to set an alarm clock, but she'd told him not to bother. "I never need an alarm, not even when I'm on early shift."

"Your call," he'd told her, being none too fond of the things, himself. The last twenty-four hours had been a real rat race. Napping through the late afternoon and waking up after dark had only screwed up his internal clock. Now, at barely 11:00 p.m., he was wiped out, but too wide-awake to fall asleep.

Switching on the radio, he searched for a news station. If she had a TV it must be in her bedroom. He'd seen no sign of one anywhere else. Personally, he could think of better things to do in a bedroom—especially hers—than watch TV.

Country music, preaching, and some nasal jerk selling an herbal cure-all. Stuff evidently worked on everything from jock itch to hiatal hernia. After a few minutes he gave up, dug his cell phone out of his jacket pocket and punched in Margaret's number. For reasons he didn't care to examine too closely, he needed grounding in reality.

After nine rings he gave up. He didn't know if she was a heavy sleeper or not, they didn't have that kind of relationship. If the guys knew he was about to marry a woman he'd never even slept with, he'd never hear the last of it. He was considered something of a connoisseur when it came to women, but they were rarely the kind of woman a man took home to meet his family. And he'd mostly quit that stuff since making up his mind to marry Margaret.

It occurred to him that it might be a good idea to invite Margaret to move in with him for a few weeks before they made it permanent. As well as he knew her—hell, they'd grown up next door—there were still a few things he didn't know about her. A lot of things, come to think of it.

He considered trying her number again on the off chance he'd woken her up with the first call, but decided against it. She was probably out of town. The decorating business involved a lot of traveling. Buying trips, trade shows, out-of-town clients.

Carson had never been particularly interested in her work, because in his family, decorators weren't needed. Furniture and paintings and such were handed down from generation to generation, a system that suited him just fine. When he'd moved out on his own, he'd taken whatever he needed from the attic. His Aunt Becky and Uncle Coley had filled in the empty spots from their attic. It was a continuity thing, passing on what was no longer needed to other family members who could make use of them. That way, nobody had to feel guilty over paying less than proper respect for the past.

He fell asleep picturing Kit, minus the purple shirt, white jeans or tie-dyed tights, sprawled across the ugly old sleigh bed he'd hauled down out of his folk's attic, that with a new mattress, suited him just fine.

Oh, yeah…

The unearthly cry came out of a dream. Carson sat up, taking only a split second to assay his surroundings. Situation awareness could save a man's life.

The penetrating cry came again, and this time he recognized it for what it was. A damned cat. If he could have located the boots he'd kicked off last night he'd have thrown both of them at the damned thing, yowling its lungs out under the front window.

Instead, he limped to the front door and let him in. "How the hell did you know where I was sleeping?" he growled as the ragged-ear tomcat wrapped himself around his bare leg.

"He knows, even when the windows are all closed. If you don't let him in he'll climb up on the roof and hang over the eaves and sing to you." Kit wandered in, rubbing her eyes.

"You call that singing?"

Instead of answering, she tipped a container of dry food into a bowl on the front porch, then poured canned milk in another bowl. "He's not my cat, he just visits occasionally. You ready for whatever?"

His eyes widened. If "whatever" included tumbling back into bed with a dewy-faced temptress wearing an oversize T-shirt he was more than ready. Early mornings were tricky for a man, especially one who'd been through a long dry spell.

"Breakfast," she said dryly. Her expression implied that she knew exactly where his mind had been. "You said last night you'd eat whatever. You can have your choice of dry cereal, leftover crab cakes from the restaurant—they're a couple of days old, so maybe you'd better not. Let's see, there's...hmm..." She stared in the open refrigerator. "Chicken soup?"

Forcefully removing his gaze from the shapely backside visible through the thin cotton knit—oh, wow, he could see the shape of everything!—Carson said gruffly, "Coffee's fine. I'd better take a look at your car before any kids start messing around with it."

She straightened up and sighed, shoving her hair away from her eyes. It obviously hadn't seen a brush recently. On the other hand, it was the kind of hair that looked pretty much the same, brushed or unbrushed.

They decided to hold off on breakfast and walk down the road instead of driving his car. That way, he figured, although he didn't voice the thought, whatever happened, they would still have one good vehicle.

"Are you sure you know what you're doing?" Kit asked when they were halfway across the front yard. She was wearing the tent-sized purple shirt and red sneakers again, completing the visual assault this time with a pair of lime green tights. Subtle, the woman was not.

"We'll soon see, won't we?"

She grabbed his arm, jerking him to a halt. "Look, if you have any doubts, let's call the sheriff. He's trained, he'll know what to do. I don't want you getting hurt on my account."

If he'd been feeling up to par he could have either laughed or taken offense. He might even have played on her fears just a little bit, ignoring for the moment his personal honor code. But he wasn't, and so he didn't. "Let me check out a few things before we call in the experts, okay."

Experts, he thought wryly, who'd probably had neither the training nor the experience that he'd had. He appreciated her concern, however. That hand-on-the-arm stuff was pretty heady.

After a walk of no more than five minutes they reached the intersection where she'd left her car. "Stand back," he said when she handed over the keys.

"Aren't you going to look first?"

"With binoculars, you mean?" he teased. "Hey, I'm looking."

Moving like a ninety-year-old man, he knelt on the dusty marl, rolled onto his back and flashed a light up underneath the chassis. Everything there checked out. After taking a moment to catch his breath, he rolled up onto his knees and pulled himself to a standing position. Wanted to tell her to turn around, to quit watching him with that look in her eyes, but he didn't.

"Next place," he muttered half to himself, "driver's side door."

Instead, he unlocked the passenger door and leaned across, searching for traces of plastic or anything the slightest bit out of alignment. He wasn't going to find anything because in the first place, she was probably paranoid, and in the second place, the guy hadn't had time to do much in plain sight of anyone who happened to be working on the waterfront a few thousand feet away.

He'd probably been checking out an abandoned car, one that might even be a collector's item. Perfectly normal reaction.

On the other hand, he'd run away when she had called

out. If he'd been interested in her car, wouldn't he have hung around to ask questions?

With Kit hovering anxiously in the background, Carson went over the vintage Beetle carefully, up and down, in and out, sniffing and testing and double checking in case he'd missed something the first time around. Wiping his hands on the seat of his khakis, it occurred to him that he was becoming entirely too familiar with the dirt around this particular intersection.

"She's okay. I'll drive her home for you," he said. "You can ride or walk, your call. We'll take my car to the sheriff's office."

"Do we have to?"

"To what, take my car?"

"Talk to the sheriff. I mean there's nothing wrong with Ladybug, so we don't really have anything more to report. The man already thinks I'm a nutcase."

She had a point. Funny thing, though—after knowing her for less than twenty-four hours, Carson was pretty sure she'd seen something. "Then let's drive out to this church of yours first. You can show me where you were when you heard the argument, when you heard the shot, and where the body was lying when you saw it."

She looked at him as if she were about to burst into tears. "You do believe me, then." It was a statement, not a question.

Something inside him twisted almost painfully. It had nothing to do with the state of his health. He held the door and she slid onto the passenger's seat. Wedging his six-foot-two frame under the steering wheel, he turned and looked at her pale profile. Funny, the way certain faces could draw a man's gaze like a magnet. "I believe you saw something," was all he was willing to admit at that point.

Back at the house, while he was waiting for Kit to do whatever she had to do to get ready, Carson ate one of the crab cakes. She was probably keeping them to feed to her critters, but he was running on empty and crab cakes were among his favorite foods.

As was just about everything else except maybe liver and strawberries. Last night's chicken soup had evidently cured what ailed him, but it lacked any real staying power.

"I'm ready," Kit said. She'd braided her hair, which made her look younger than ever. Carson told himself he ought to be ashamed of the lecherous thoughts that kept sneaking into his mind. Hell, he was practically a married man. Besides, he was old enough to be her…uncle.

She snagged a straw hat and a pair of oversized, orange-framed sunglasses. His mother would have loved the hat. Both the crown and half the brim were covered with big, frowsy fake flowers.

"If I'd known it was going to be formal, I'd have brought along a tie," he quipped, ushering her out the door.

Unassisted, she climbed up into the four-wheel drive vehicle without comment. Margaret always made an issue of his choice of wheels, claiming it was a juvenile hold-over from his days playing at being a NASCAR driver.

She was probably right, but he liked to think it was more a practical choice than a matter of testosterone. He lived in the sticks, after all. Some of his favorite fishing spots weren't exactly on the beaten track.

"Wow, I really like this thing," Kit commented, wriggling her shapely behind on the bucket seat. She twisted around to look over the spacious cargo area. "It would hold practically every thing I own, Ladybug included."

"Comes in handy. I live out in the country." Something else Margaret held against him. They still had a few issues to settle before they tied the knot. "You want to point me in the right direction?"

She leaned forward and turned on the radio, touching first one button, then another. "My mother drove a Mercedes. That is, she lost her license, but we still had it when..." She cut her eyes at him, those rain-soft, laser-sharp gray eyes that seemed to see right through him. "This is a lot more practical, though. You probably won't believe me, but I'm actually extremely practical."

Yeah, right. A woman who drove a thirty-five-year-old car that held roughly the same amount of cargo as a road bike. "You want to clue me in on where we're going?"

And while you're at it, stop wriggling around on my front seat, smelling like sugar and spice and everything nice. I don't need the distraction, he added silently.

She faced forward, all business. "Go past the wharf and take a left. It's not paved, but it's usually passable unless we've had lots of rain or the wind's blown the water up the creeks." After a while she said, "Jeff says the village used to be a lot bigger than it is now. His family's been here forever. Now, though, about the only thing left out in this area we're going to is the church, the cemetery, a few old ruined houses and some sunken boats." She twisted around and flashed that guileless grin that made her look too damned young. That and the freckles and the braid. "That's what makes it so perfect for *Gretchen's Ghost,*" she said ingenuously.

"Uh-huh."

In the ten minutes or so it took to get there, she told him about the work in progress and about *Claire the Loon,* which had been optioned for TV, but probably wouldn't make the cut. Carson found himself intrigued by the way the woman's mind worked. He told her she could probably look at a rock and make up a story about it.

She looked thoughtful for a moment, but didn't deny it.

And then they were at the old church. Boarded-up windows, leaning steeple, weeds growing up through the graveled parking lot. Off to one side stood several makeshift tables in various stages of disrepair, used in bygone days, no doubt, for dinner-on-the-ground meetings.

He deliberately parked off the road near the entrance to the parking lot in case there were any tracks worth examining. If a deputy had checked out the scene, that meant there'd be at least one more set of tracks obliterating the evidence. As for anything else, he didn't hold out a lot of hope. Usually in a case where a body went missing, a certain level of professionalism was indicated.

Which made Kit's situation all the more precarious, he reminded himself, one hand on the door as he scanned the peaceful scene. Anyone who took the time to remove the body was unlikely to allow a potential witness to go free.

"It's nice, isn't it? I mean other than…you know." He could hear the brittle edge in her voice. She had obviously tried hard to convince herself that she'd been mistaken, but it hadn't worked. The lady had definitely heard something she wasn't meant to hear and seen something she wasn't meant to see, and as he was the only one who believed her at the moment, it was up to him to protect her.

Carson was half tempted to bring up the reason he had tracked her down just to get it out of the way. Knowing something of what his cousin Lance had gone through trying to convince Liza that he wasn't trying to pull a con when he'd offered her ten Gs and a chunk of worthless certificates, he was tempted to rush through the spiel while Kit was still too distracted to argue.

He'd already wasted what—two days? Three? By the time he'd reached North Carolina he'd been too damned miserable to track time with any degree of accuracy. The fact that he had yet to mention the yellowed, bug-eaten, all-but-illegible stock certificates and the check with her name on it said a lot about his inability to focus.

She could obviously use the money. Hell, she didn't even own a TV. So why not just hand off, head south and get on with the next thing on his agenda? He still had a few more days on disability, plus a lot of unused leave. He could stretch it a few more days if he had to, but sooner or later he needed to get on with his own life.

Kit slid out of the car and he moved around to stand beside her. "Right over there," she said, pointing to a general area near the center of a weedy, poorly graveled surface designed to hold maybe a dozen cars. "That's where the body was. I thought at first it was a deer or a big dog." She shuddered. Without thinking, he put his arm around her. She was stiff at first, but he sensed a yielding. A reluctant yielding, as if she didn't want to give in to her own worst fears.

They stood like that for a couple of minutes while he studied the alleged crime scene, filing away the details for later evaluation. Not that there was much to see. No yellow tape, that was for damned sure. Some low scrub, mostly groundsel, yaupon and wax myrtle. Thanks to his mother, he knew his shrubbery, cultivated and otherwise. Beyond that was the usual wetland growth, mostly bulrushes, with the invasive phragmites starting to move in and a creek winding in from the nearby Currituck Sound.

Kit started to move out onto the parking lot, but he caught her arm and pulled her back, not wanting her to compromise any possible evidence. Somehow, her back ended up pressed against his chest, her bottom against his groin. For a moment neither of them moved, but he didn't miss the sharp intake of her breath. Carson told himself he was holding her back only because he didn't want her trampling any possible evidence.

Speaking of evidence, there was no way she could miss the evidence of his body's involuntary reaction, which could be described as enthusiastic, inappropriate, unwanted and damned embarrassing.

"Do you see what I see?" In an effort to distract her, he pointed toward the center of the area in question. "Look it over—tell me what strikes you as odd." He stepped back, giving her time to recover—giving them both time.

"Well…some of the weeds are bent over," she said thoughtfully. "Like they'd been raked or something," she added after a moment.

"But just in one narrow area."

"Like something was dragged across," she said, picking up on his line of thought.

"Right. To just about where we're standing now."

Kit glanced down at her feet, then looked at him over her shoulder. "Are we messing up evidence?"

"I doubt it. Tracks of at least two cars have been here recently."

"Mine?"

He shook his head. They were standing side by side now, a safe few feet apart, facing the old Primitive Baptist church with its leaning steeple. Kit's hands were on her hips, her feet spread in a take-no-prisoners stance. Her braid was already relinquishing control of her curly auburn hair.

Dammit, he didn't need this kind of a distraction, not now.

Not ever, a dutiful conscience reminded him.

"Since yours. One was a standard-size sedan." A patrol car, he figured. "You said the sheriff had driven out to investigate?"

"Someone from the department did. I guess that's why they were so angry. They didn't find anything."

"I figure the other vehicle for a pickup truck, which narrows it down to maybe a hundred or so possibilities just in the immediate vicinity. With no leads, there's no way of narrowing it down further."

"What about that funny sound I heard when whoever fired the shot drove off? I told you about it, didn't I?"

"Right. A muffler pack narrows the suspects down to maybe a few dozen. Offhand, I'd say roughly three out of every five vehicles in this area are pickup trucks or SUVs." Carson moved onto the graveled lot, waving for her to stay behind him. Unless he got lucky, without forensics he couldn't prove much except that a certain area had been disturbed while all the rest remained pretty much untouched except where a vehicle—probably Kit's Ladybug—had driven over it. Something—or someone—had been dragged away from roughly the center of the parking lot. The area could have been raked to cover any bloodstains that might have soaked into the surface, but depending on the caliber, the slug was probably still inside the victim's head. Odds were that no shell casing would be found, but if he could rent a metal detector, he might make a few sweeps.

Dammit, he shouldn't have to do this. That's what the local law was for. He should never have gotten mixed up in it in the first place.

She was watching him closely with those unsettling eyes. Either he was reading too much into a simple gaze, or she was sending messages he was in no shape to receive.

Or the message was scrambled and he lacked the key to translate.

Probably just waiting for him to follow her on a tour. "All right, show me this cemetery," he said, wishing he were in his own jurisdiction. Wishing he knew more about the local law.

Wishing the woman herself weren't so damned distracting.

Six

It was nearing noon when they completed the tour. Carson had wanted to drive directly to the sheriff's office, but when he'd called to get directions he'd been told Sheriff Mayhew was in Raleigh at a meeting of the Sheriff's Association, and that both deputies were away from the office.

"I told you it wouldn't do any good," Kit said, wandering in with two napkin-wrapped sandwiches. Offering him one, she said, "Feta cheese and dandelion greens on whole wheat with salsa and ripe olives."

He peeled back a flap of napkin and eyed the thing warily. "I'm, uh—not particularly hungry."

"You need to eat to regain your strength. I saw you limping out there. You might not have sneezed all day, but you can't tell me you're not suffering from something. Is your head still hurting?"

He shook it. It didn't fall off, so he told her he was

fine, just fine. Her gaze slid down his body, centering on his knees. He was still wearing the pants he'd worn yesterday, mud-stains and all. He'd brought along a second pair of khakis just in case, along with a clean shirt and a decent jacket, but he was keeping those for emergencies.

Although after what he'd been through so far, he didn't even want to think about what might constitute an emergency. "I don't usually eat weeds."

"Don't know what you're missing. Try it, you might like it. If you don't, you can pull out the greenery."

He took a bite. She settled onto one of the kitchen chairs and he hooked the other one and sat. The stuff wasn't too bad. At least, if it was, the salsa was hot enough to cover the damage, not to mention cauterizing any flu germs that might be hanging around.

"Uh—I don't think I'm contagious," he felt obliged to say. At least he wasn't unless he gave in to any wild impulses.

Rising stiffly, he poured them both a glass of milk, then turned to find her eyes focused on his nether regions again. Before he could question her interest, she laid down her sandwich and said, "You're still limping. I didn't hit you all that hard, did I?"

"You didn't." Hadn't hit him at all, but he wasn't above using her conscience to his advantage. "Most of the damage was already done, but I might've twisted something when I jumped out of the way."

"What damage? Tell me about it."

Like she cared about his health. Still, all things considered she'd been pretty decent. "You know—the usual. Bad cold now—accident a few weeks back. Aren't you even curious about how I knew who you were?"

"What usual? Your bungee cord was too long? You leap tall buildings without a safety net?"

"Enough about me. Look, admit it—you were scared stiff when I called you by your full name. Aren't you even going to ask how I knew?"

She frowned, then shook her head and took another bite. When she was able, she said, "I panicked when I thought you'd come to silence me, but now that I know you didn't, I figure it has something to do with either my folks or my books. But you're from South Carolina, not Virginia, so it's probably the books. Not that I'm a celebrity or anything like that—I mean, I've done a few autograph sessions, but there are plenty of really well-known authors right here on the Outer Banks. Gilbert's Point isn't actually part of the banks, but you know what I mean."

He didn't, but he was willing to let her ramble since it was what she did best. If he could sift through half of what she said and match up a word here and there, he might have a clue as to what she was all about.

Then again, he might not.

"Wait here, I want to show you something," he said. Laying his half-eaten sandwich aside, he rose and headed for the living room where he'd left his briefcase. Just as he reached for it, his cell phone rang.

There were times when he wished the coverage weren't so damned good.

Identifying the number as Margaret's, he said, "Yeah, what's wrong?" She rarely called him unless there was a last minute change of plans.

There was a last minute change of plans.

"The hell you say," he muttered, leaning against the doorframe.

From the kitchen, Kit was staring at him, her eyes questioning. "What's wrong? she mouthed.

"Listen, Maggie, can it wait until I get home? Mom's all right, isn't she? You didn't tell her—"

Kit came and stood beside him and he reached out absently and hauled her closer. "Listen, don't make a move until I get home, will you just promise me that much? Your friend can wait another few days, can't he?"

Kit didn't say a word, but feeling her surprisingly sturdy body beside him felt good. Damn good. He broke the connection and held back on expressing himself. His mama had taught him better than to use foul language in the presence of a lady. "Okay, you want some answers? We'll trade. You wouldn't happen to have any beer on hand, would you?"

She shook her head. "I don't keep anything alcoholic in case I'm allergic."

That pulled his attention away from his immediate problem. "Allergic to beer? The hops, you mean?"

"My mother was an alcoholic," she said with grave dignity. "I think maybe her father might have been one, too, I'm not sure. I don't really remember Mama's family."

Carson rubbed the back of his neck. "Coffee, then. Strong."

While she measured out grounds and set the pot to brewing, he paced the small kitchen, sifting through various mental files in order of priority. Then, while the pot did its burbling duty, he straddled a chair and started talking in no particular order.

Evidently the style was contagious.

"I looked you up on a chart—tracked you down mostly through your cousin. By the way, she says you owe her a call or at least an e-mail."

Kit perched on the bar stool—she had only the one. It didn't match anything else in the room. "Liza? How do you know her? I don't do computer things."

"Like I told you, didn't I? She married my cousin. I guess that makes us cousins, right?"

Kissing cousins. The thought popped into her mind out of nowhere. Kit tried not to let his wickedly attractive grin affect her. When on earth had her life gone so completely off the rails? She really, really needed to be in control, and right now she wasn't even in control of her own kitchen.

"Wrong," she said. "I don't even know you. I have no idea what you're doing here except that I might have caused you an injury and you're obviously sick, and—well, I guess I needed someone and you just happened along, but I don't need you any longer."

The grin didn't fade. If anything, it got even wider. Truly extraordinary eyes, she thought disjointedly. She needed to get rid of him—he was the last thing she needed, the very last. "Look, if you've got something to say, then spit it out. I've got a lot to do and I don't even know where to start."

He raised his eyebrows in a way that sucked the words out of her before she could stop the flow. "Okay, so I do know. First I need to make the sheriff believe me, and then I've got to figure out how to stay alive, and then there's my grandparents." She clapped a hand over her mouth. With a stricken look, she whispered, "Oh, for Heaven's sake, the anniversary party!"

"Lucent as ever," he said. "Good to know you haven't lost your chain of thought."

"Oh—bull!"

"That about sums it up," he said, the grin fading.

That two-day growth of beard had to be a fashion statement, Kit thought despairingly. On him, it was lethal.

"All right, so now you know my story. Now it's your turn. Why did you come looking for me?"

"To give you ten thousand dollars."

Her mouth fell open. She snapped it shut, glaring at him. "Right. And your name is Ed Thingamabob—you know who I mean. And you're going to tell me I just won the sweepstakes, right?"

He sighed as if he was running short of patience. "Look, it's easy if you'll just listen and not make any judgment until I'm finished. In case you hadn't heard, your cousin Liza jumped to the wrong conclusion and Lance had one hell of a time trying to persuade her he was on the level."

The cousin thing again—she'd almost forgotten. There was obviously some connection between them, but cousinhood was not the relationship she'd have preferred, given a choice.

Oh, and what would you prefer?

Don't ask, she thought, quelling a rush of something that felt dangerously like arousal.

Lips clamped tightly together, she waited for him to continue.

Sprawling in the chair, with one elbow propped on her table, he did. "Listen, at the moment I've got a lot on my mind. I don't have time to hold you down and convince you." Her imagination flared at the thought. "Just take my word for it, I owe you the money—maybe a lot more, but ten K is all I can scrape up without liquidating a few investments, and with the market on a downward spiral—"

She hopped down off the stool and grabbed her head with both hands. "Stop! Just stop right there, I don't know what you're trying to pull, but you don't owe me any-thing! Cousin or not, I never even saw you before yesterday, so if you don't mind, how about just moving on. My life at the moment is complicated enough without any—any slow-walking, smooth-talking stranger offering me candy. I wasn't born yesterday, you know.''

He arched a dark brow at that, and she could have bitten her tongue. Speak first, think later—if ever. You'd think she would learn after awhile.

The errant eyebrow settled back into place and he looked so discouraged she nearly gave in. That was the last thing she could afford to do. In less than twenty-four hours she had discovered a weakness she'd never even known she had.

A weakness for blue-eyed men with square, grizzled jaws and twisty grins—with hard, lean bodies and a soft-spoken take-command attitude that rubbed her the wrong way and the right way, at the same time. It didn't even make sense. She wasn't about to allow anyone to take control of her life, no matter how appealing he was. She had good reason to know what happened when a woman gave up control, and it wasn't going to happen to her, no way, no how.

She opened her mouth to speak, but he beat her to it. ''Listen, Kit, it's not what you think. Just give me another minute, all right? Go back with me a few generations.''

Gladly, a romantic, irresponsible element whispered.

''Your great-great-grandfather—I think—lent some money to my great-great-grandfather. You with me so far?''

Ignoring the whisper, she crossed her arms over her breasts and stared him down, daring him to convince her of anything.

''My grandfather—his name, in case it matters, was Lancelot Beckett—the first of several, actually. Anyhow, at the time all this got started, his family had lost everything in the War Between the States and he was having a hard time getting back on his feet. The Becketts had been in banking before the war. To make a long story short, old Lance did a favor for an Oklahoma cowboy named Chandler, who, according to a genealogical chart we commissioned, was your great-great-grandfather. You still with me?''

Grudgingly, she nodded, her interest growing in spite of herself. She wished old Cast Iron could hear this, whether or not it was true. He'd always claimed the Chandlers were trash, her mother the trashiest of the lot, and she didn't know enough about that side of her family to disprove the charge.

''So—where was I? Chandler gave old Lance some money to invest, but by the time the investment paid off, Chandler had disappeared. The Becketts went on to prosper, but they never found out what had happened to the cowboy. He never got in touch again, and unfortunately, the debt never got repaid. So that's where the ten grand comes in. There's a bundle of stock and some old letters, but they're worthless and almost impossible to pry apart, much less to read. A hundred years in an attic under a leaky roof can do that.''

He waited.

She waited.

The coffeepot signaled its readiness, and Kit turned and took down two mugs. She plopped them down on the counter, poured, and set out a can of fat free evaporated milk and a sugar bowl filled with brown sugar.

Carson accepted the coffee, declined the rest and waited for her to argue. He inhaled suspiciously. The woman was evidently some kind of a health nut. For all he knew, the coffee might be roasted acorns or something equally disgusting, but it smelled all right. Damned good, in fact.

"Who's Margaret?" she asked out of the blue.

He choked on the coffee—it was the real thing—and set his mug down. "She, uh—she's my fiancée. Sort of."

"Sort of? What kind of an answer is that?"

"Look, it's not important right now. We need to settle two things, and then I'll get out of your hair. First, I've got a cashier's check and the stock—you might as well have it, no one else wants it. Maybe you can sell it to an antique dealer. Next, I'll stop by the sheriff's office on my way out of town and try and convince him that a crime's been committed, and that you need some protection until things are cleared up."

"You're leaving, then?"

The sound of a distant siren wove through the room like an errant breeze. The front door was open; it was that kind of day. Fickle March.

"Yeah, it seems I've got this situation at home that needs handling."

"Does it have something to do with your sort-of fiancée?"

So then, without intending to, Carson found himself telling her what was going on down in Charleston. About his mother and her wedding fixation, and his decision to marry while she was still able to take part. "I'm thirty-seven years old, never been married—I'm a cop," he said with a shrug. "That makes me a pretty lousy risk. Margaret understands, though. She grew up next door, and she happens to love my mother."

"And you?"

Without answering, he rose and moved to look out the window. "Something's going on down by the wharf. An unmarked and an ambulance just pulled in."

"Unmarked what?"

He turned then to look at her, and wished he hadn't.

Wide gray eyes, freckles, frowsy hair—both white-knuckled hands gripping her coffee mug. The combination of gutsiness and vulnerability was bad enough. Throw in a kind of sexuality that was all the more effective because it was—he was almost sure of it—totally unintentional, and you had a major hazard.

"An unmarked car," he said, dragging his thoughts back in line. "At a guess, one of your deputies. Want to go see what's happening? Might be some connection to your churchyard murder."

He watched as she visibly braced herself. Shoulders back, head up. Oh yeah, she was a spunky lady.

"Let me get my shoes on."

"You got a key for this place?"

On her way to the bedroom, she glanced over her shoulder. "A key? Why would I need a key? It's outside, over the doorframe. I guess."

"Figures," he said dryly.

For a woman who'd just witnessed a murder and claimed to be scared out of her gourd someone was trying to blow up her car or otherwise do her bodily injury, she was incredibly dumb.

Make that naïve, he thought as he retrieved the key.

The hubbub down at the waterfront had expanded until he figured the entire village and half the county had migrated there within the past few minutes.

Kit had thrown on a blue-and-orange plaid sweater over the purple shirt, along with the red shoes and green tights. It had to be deliberate. Not even color blindness could account for that degree of outrageousness. He had an idea it was her version of a red cape flaunted before the world. *Here I am, folks—take your best shot.*

Seven

"**E**el fisherman. Old guy, name of Tank Hubble," Jeff Matlock said quietly, his gaze on Kit, who was standing near the fringes of the crowd talking to the other waitress. Evidently, all the businesses—all five of them—had turned out. "Lived alone. Nobody reported him missing."

"You got any idea what happened?" Carson asked quietly. "He drowned?"

"Maybe. Hole in his head didn't help, though."

"So he was shot," Carson said softly. "Once? More than once?"

A single gunshot, Kit had said.

"All I seen was one. Hard to tell what caliber—it weren't a shotgun, that's for sure." Jeff had evidently been one of the first ones on the scene after a local fisherman had brought in the body that was just now being bagged. "Been in the water a while. Crabs was just starting in on him."

Carson digested the information, processing it into what he already knew. Which was too damned little. "Who found him?"

"Couple of kids. They was messing around in Martha's Creek when they saw something floating up from under an eel pot. Turned out, it was ol' Tank's shirttail. One of the kids called his pappy, and he went and brought him in. Been me, I'd've called Billy or Mooney."

"Billy or Mooney," Carson repeated.

"Deputies. Billy, he's local. Mooney, he comes from somewhere up north. Been here a couple of months. Seems like a nice kid, though."

Nice didn't cut it. Smart would have been better. From where they were standing, Carson could see the two uniformed deputies talking to a couple of school-age kids. One of the boys was talking; the other looked as if he'd just been sick and was about to offer up an encore.

Gulls circled overhead, adding to the noise level. The smell of diesel fuel mingled with the effluvia of fish-cleaning tables, shell heaps and deep-frying grease. Carson took it all in—the sounds, the sights, the smells. He was tempted to wander over, flash his credentials and see what he could learn, but small-town law had a way of being territorial.

So did big-town law, for that matter, but he had a feeling this one might spill over into DEA territory before it was over.

He also had a feeling the restaurateur might know more than he was saying. Smart man. He had to live around these parts, and Carson was a stranger. Had Kit confided in her boss last night when she'd gone to work? And if so, to what extent?

Carson reminded himself that this wasn't his case. Every few minutes Jeff's gaze would stray over to where the two waitresses were talking. Carson didn't have to wonder which of them he was watching. The pocket Venus, Bimbo or Babette—whatever she called herself—was easily enough to attract a second look. But Kit was...

She was simply Kit. Outrageous, elegant, flaky, flamboyant. Add to that gutsy and vulnerable and it still wasn't the sum total of the woman he'd driven some four hundred miles to find.

Trouble was, now that he'd found her, he wasn't quite sure what to do with her. He knew what he'd like to do with her.

Oh, yeah.

The ambulance pulled away, sans sirens. The crowd showed no sign of dispersing. More than once Carson heard the word drugs being whispered. Like any interstate highway that ran roughly north and south, the inland waterway was a convenient conduit.

These people might live in the backwoods, but that didn't mean they weren't aware of what went on in the world. Not only did they have ready access to information, but living in the slow lane they had more time to process that information. To ponder, as PawPaw would've said. Country wisdom wasn't entirely a myth.

Had Hubble been a bit player? Or had he simply been in the wrong place at the wrong time? Seen or heard something he wasn't supposed to see or hear? The proverbial innocent bystander.

Like Kit. The way things were shaping up she was definitely at risk if she was even suspected of having been on the scene.

A pelican settled heavily on top of a post near the end of the wharf to size up the crowd, gauging his chances for a handout. With a brief nod to the other man, Carson turned away, his eyes instinctively searching for a familiar purple shirt.

Well, hell. Like he needed this. With a mother who was disappearing deeper into her own world every day, a fiancée who was on her way to New York to discuss hooking up with an established interior design firm, and a check he was obligated to deliver that the recipient didn't seem interested in accepting, he really didn't need another problem. Not to mention the fact that his bones weren't healing as fast as they had ten years ago, or even five.

He'd been fifteen the first time he'd broken a bone. He'd been seventeen the first time he'd gotten drunk— even younger than that when he'd discovered what sex was all about.

Meanwhile, not quite a generation apart, but close, little Kitty Dixon had been drawing stick figures and making up ghost stories to entertain her kindergarten pals.

He caught a drift of some faint spicy fragrance an instant before she came up behind him and hooked her arm through his. "I told you so," she murmured. "Do you believe me now?"

Her touch made him suck in his breath. "I believed you all along," he lied.

In unspoken alliance they turned toward her house, following the weed-bordered footpath past a few dockside sheds, a thicket of wild plum that was just now starting to bloom and a vacant house that had evidently been used for target practice a time or two.

A place like this could grow on you, Carson mused.

Yeah, like moss. Like a fungus.

"Sure you don't want to talk to the deputies before they leave?" he felt obligated to ask. "They'd probably listen to you now."

"They had their chance. Besides, this is turning real ugly—I'm not sure I want to get involved after all."

"Murder's always ugly." Still, he couldn't much blame her for wanting to back off. She was a woman alone, with no visible support system.

An anxious expression clouding her eyes, she said, "Is it all right? I mean I was a witness...sort of. Is there some law that says I have to keep going back until they're willing to listen?"

Carson considered the extent of his own obligations as a fellow law officer. He had a choice. He could tell her what she wanted to hear—that she'd made the effort and been rebuffed, which ended her duty as a citizen—or he could he tell her what she didn't want to hear, but needed to: that anyone with any knowledge of a crime had a duty to come forward. If she'd left her name they could have found her for any further questioning.

He waited until they'd reached the single section of picket fence in front of her house where she parked her car, to make up his mind. To hell with duty. He was off-duty now, not to mention way out of his jurisdiction.

They gravitated toward the kitchen, and a few minutes later they were seated at the table, mugs of reheated coffee in hand, more for comfort than stimulation. Under that big, bold shirt, she looked too fragile. He'd already explained about the condition of the stock certificates, but he hadn't had time to show her the letter that had been handed down through the generations that was supposed to explain it all. Written in faded ink in an elegant hand his mother had referred to as copperplate, it was all but impossible to decipher after an army of insects had helped themselves. Still, it might prove just the distraction she needed.

He brought in his briefcase, opened it and set the stuff

out on the table between them. It even smelled old. "I've already explained what this is all about," he said.

Had he? So much had happened in so short a time, damned if he could remember what he'd told her and what he'd only rehearsed in his mind. "The rest of this stuff is pretty much window dressing, but the check's good. It was cut less than a week ago, so you see—"

"What day is this?" Kit asked suddenly.

Puzzled, Carson glanced at his watch. "Uh...Friday."

"Oh, shoot!" She jumped up, leaving the check and documents on the red-enameled table.

Carson raked back his chair to follow. "Kit? Is something wrong?" Her bedroom door was open. He followed her inside.

She was standing in front of her open closet, scowling at the contents. "This week has been just plain crazy. Or maybe it's psychological. Do you think that's it? Like I didn't want to remember, and so even though I kept reminding myself, when the time came, I forgot?"

Off into the wild blue yonder again, Carson thought, half-bemused. He was fairly certain the woman had a full complement of gray cells, but either there was a short circuit somewhere along the line or a few of her dipswitches needed attention.

"You want to give me a hint?"

"A hint? Oh—the party. I told you."

He nodded as if he understood exactly what she was talking about. "Right. The party."

Gradually, as if a hologram were taking shape around him, he became aware of his surroundings. Her bedroom walls were the kind of old-fashioned paneling called beaded ceiling. The color of strong tea, it had never seen a lick of paint. Instead of the wild colors and patterns he might have expected, the accessories were plain white cotton, from the curtains that graced the two tall, double-hung windows to the bedspread that covered the single bed, to the cheap scatter rugs on the worn pine floors.

And while the décor was the last thing he would have expected, the scent that lingered there was hers alone. Fruity, spicy, with a hint of something that reminded him of his mother's flower border.

While he watched, she reached inside the closet and brought forth a dress made of some slithery material, the color and pattern so bright he almost flinched. She eyed it critically, as if trying to make up her mind about something. If she offered him a vote, it would be a resounding negative. The thing was neither red nor purple but somewhere in between, covered with flowers roughly the size of hubcaps.

She held it up in front of her and turned this way and that, examining her image in the oval dresser mirror, like a little girl playing dress up.

Only Kit wasn't a little girl. And what he'd like to play with her wasn't dress up, it was more like undress.

Could a broken leg affect the brain?

Obviously it could. He'd outgrown hotwired hormones about ten years ago.

"I caught my heel in the hem the last time I wore my black and I never got around to mending it," she said as if that explained everything.

Wrenching his eyes away from her backside, where her shirt was hiked up over those tights, he looked down at her red sneakers, then at the dress she was still clutching against her body.

Oh, no, he thought. You wouldn't....

Yeah, she probably would. And on her, it would probably work. Like whatsername, the actress who'd worn orange sneakers with a black designer gown to the Emmy Awards a few years ago.

Make that a few decades ago, he thought ruefully.

"Look, I've got to shower. I don't suppose you brought a suit with you, did you?"

"Huh?" Totally bemused, he shook his head. "Sorry. Clean pair of khakis, blue shirt and navy blazer. I wasn't sure what I was going to be dealing with when I left home."

"It'll do. You want the first shower, or me? My hair takes longer to dry, but if I use the dryer it frizzes up all over."

If she wanted to blame it on her dryer, that was all right with him. Personally, he sort of liked it. "Go ahead, then, I'll wait. What shall I do with your check?"

"My what? Oh, that. Put it in the refrigerator, will you? I'll have to think about whether or not I'm going to accept it."

"The refrigerator," he repeated, not sure he'd heard her correctly.

Beam me up, Scotty.

"Well, it's metal and insulated, in case the house burns down before we get back."

Before we get back. Right.

Impatiently, she said, "Look, I don't have a safe, so if you're worried about your check, put it in the freezer compartment."

It's *your* check, dammit, he wanted to say, but didn't. Wouldn't do any good. She was switched onto transmit now, not receive.

Jerking open a dresser drawer, she grabbed a handful of underwear. Surprisingly enough, it was plain white, too, just like her bedroom accessories. Carson decided he'd been right about one thing, at least. Kit Dixon was making a statement.

Now all he had to do was figure out who the recipient was supposed to be—the world at large, or someone in particular.

Correction: he didn't have to figure out a damned thing. It was none of his business.

A few hours later he had his first clue as to what might have provoked her aggressive-defensive attitude. Her grandfather, the judge, was a type he recognized, having testified in a number of court cases over the years. The man was biased, opinionated, with a mind set in concrete that had long since hardened. The law was whatever the judge said it was on a given day. Argue and find yourself in contempt.

"And you are—?" The portly old guy in the three-piece suit and old-fashioned ribbon tie deliberately stepped just inside what Carson considered his personal space. Kit had been swept away by three older women, hastily introduced as friends of her grandmother.

Judge Abner Andrew Dixon looked him over as if he were peering through a magnifying glass. He didn't offer to shake hands.

"Carson Beckett, sir. Friend of your granddaughter's, up visiting from South Carolina."

"South C'lina, hmm? How did you meet my grand-daughter?"

Bracing himself for cross-examination, Carson decided the money was none of the old despot's business. He had a feeling there were issues between Kit and her grand-father that wouldn't be helped by any explanations he could make.

"Kit's cousin married mine last summer. She might have mentioned it?"

Bushy white eyebrows lowered, the judge took a moment to ruminate. "Must be on her mother's side," he dismissed.

Carson nodded.

"Thought so." His sour expression spoke volumes. And without another word, the old gent wheeled and left.

Both amused and irritated, Carson remained for several minutes between the entrance hall door and a Kentucky Derby-sized flower arrangement, watching as well-dressed and obviously well-heeled guests merged and broke apart to circulate, only to merge and circulate again. Aside from one or two curious glances, few paid him any attention, which suited him just fine.

Although he wasn't exactly dressed for it, Carson felt comfortable enough. His own family no longer did much entertaining, but he'd attended his share of such events back when his uncle Coley had been active in politics.

He nodded to the few people who offered him tentative smiles. They were obviously trying to place him, trying to figure out if he was someone important. Probably figured if he was confident enough to show up tieless at what was not quite a black-tie affair, but almost, then he must be someone important.

From time to time he caught sight of Kit, usually with a tall, well-dressed guy in tow. The guy reminded him of an actor whose name he couldn't recall. Once she'd given him a little finger wave, her expression one of silent commiseration. At a guess, he'd say she was having about as much fun as he was. Better than a dental appointment, but not much.

Who the hell was the guy who kept following her

around, hovering over her like an Armani-clad guardian angel?

Leaning against the only spot on the wall that wasn't covered by furniture, flowers or a gilt-framed portrait of some grim-faced ancestor, Carson sized up the crowd. Roughly three-quarters of them he figured for lawyers— well-dressed, well-schooled, a few of them already well lubricated. Among the remainder were probably a few politicians, as they usually stemmed from the same source. Spouses, naturally, all monotonously suitably dressed, with pearls and black crepe predominating. Now and then a red dress, but nothing even close to that horror Kit was wearing.

God love her, she was something else.

For the third time since they'd arrived, Carson checked his watch. Seventeen minutes. Twenty was his minimum, forty his maximum, but then, this was Kit's gig, not his. He braced his feet apart and continued to take in the scene before him as if it were a crime scene he was trying to get a read on. Old habits died hard.

He was beginning to get a fix on the enigma that was Kit Dixon. The judge had obviously disapproved of her mother—in which case, loyalty alone might have forced Kit to strike out on her own after both parents had died.

What about her father, the judge's son? Where did he fit in? Give the man some credit; he'd chosen to marry Elizabeth Chandler, hadn't he? Carson was biased toward the Chandlers, if only for what they'd done to jump-start the Becketts after the war. Then, too, he thought a lot of Lance's wife, who'd been born a Chandler.

He was tempted to ask Kit about her parents—that is, he might if he were going to be here long enough. She might even give him an answer. Then again, she might give him a response straight out of *Star Wars* or some

Disney epic. Whoever she was—whatever drove her, Kit Dixon lived in a unique universe all her own.

Actually, the dress wasn't all that bad, now that he was used to it. Earlier that evening, she'd emerged from her bedroom about the same time he'd opened the bathroom door. He'd still been trying to brush a few wrinkles out of his best khakis and wishing he'd thought to bring along another pair of shoes.

He distinctly remembered gaping. The coat hanger hadn't done justice to the dress. Hubcap-sized blossoms and all, it was…something else. Sleeveless, cut straight across her collarbone, it skimmed her body, clinging to a few points of interest along the way, like breasts and hip-bones, to swirl around her ankles.

Her ankles. Delicate didn't begin to describe them. If Occupational Safety and Health Administration ever got a look at those shoes she was almost wearing—four-inch heels, a paper-thin sole and a single narrow band across the toes—she'd be in real trouble.

Even thinking about her, his gaze unconsciously homed in on her location across the crowded room. She was moving. He'd noticed that about her before—that even when she was standing still, some part of her body was always moving. Shoulders, hands—a tapping foot.

Was she as impatient with this whole tea party as he was?

At the moment she was talking to a rake-thin blonde in a black dress whose ankles, incidentally, were almost as fine. Without taking time to think, Carson levered his way from the wall that had been supporting him and headed across the room.

"'scuse me. Oops, sorry." He was halfway there before he noticed the well-dressed Ralph Fiennes type standing a few feet away, but clearly a part of the small group. Kit happened to look up and catch his eye. Either he was crazy, or she was trying to send him a message.

Back off? Get me out of here?

Oh, good, he was coming to rescue her. Tired beyond belief, Kit allowed the words to flow around her. She was good at tuning out. She'd been doing it all her life for one reason or another.

"Isn't that right, Katherine?" her grandmother asked, and she smiled and nodded like one of those silly bobble dolls.

Get it together, she told herself sternly.

Of course, she told herself that on the average of twice a day. And so far, she'd managed to do just that, but recent events had shattered any gains she might have made toward maintaining a quiet, orderly lifestyle.

"You remember that movie, don't you, Katherine? I think you must have been about twelve at the time. I remember telling your mother that you were too young to see it."

She hadn't a clue which movie her grandmother was talking about. She had never been too young. Sometimes she thought she'd been born old. But she smiled and nodded again. Another five minutes and her duty would be done for the next six months. If she failed to show up for six years, her absence probably wouldn't even be noticed, but her conscience would nag her. Her conscience was like a five-pound anchor—not big enough to do much good, just big enough to be a drag.

"I got it at Bergdorf's for half the price." The voices wafted around her while she counted down the seconds before she could politely make her escape. Come on, Carson, sweep me off my feet and get me out of here!

"Oh, this? Antoine said it was the last thing he designed before he died, can you imagine? I simply had to have it, of course.'' The speaker wore a black dress no different from two thirds of the women present. It amused Kit to see how her grandmother's friends deliberately avoided commenting on what Kit had chosen to wear.

Why do you keep on doing it? her five-pound anchor of a conscience demanded.

Because it drives my grandfather up a wall, she told herself with grim satisfaction.

She felt sorry for her grandmother, she honestly did, but then, she was what the shrinks called an enabler. All those years she had stood silently by while the two Dixon men, father and son, had taunted poor Elizabeth Chandler, whose only faults were a tendency toward addictive behavior and rotten taste in husbands. Taunted her into alcoholism, which had led—at least, in Kit's estimation— to an indiscreet affair that had given them even more ammunition.

And all the while, their precious, perfect son had been so coldly abusive to both his wife and his daughter that even now Kit still woke up occasionally in the middle of the night, desperately seeking light and air. Being locked in a closet for hours on end left a lasting impression. Once she'd been confined for more than twenty-four hours when her father had been delayed in court and her mother had been in an alcoholic stupor.

Now Kit shifted her weight to the other foot. Mercy, these shoes ought to be against the law! She took a deep breath, looking around the familiar room in the bayside mansion some three-quarters of a mile from where she had grown up. It all came down to money. Money and position. Grandmother Dixon had had both; grandfather Dixon had had neither. Once they'd been married, it had all become his.

Money had strings, Kit reminded herself. Which was why she continued to flaunt her independence before the old man she had learned to despise before she'd even learned to ride her first two-wheeler. If he thought he could dangle her inheritance before her now and make her jump to his tune, he was sadly mistaken. She had a roof over her head—she had clothes to wear—she had books on her shelf that she had written herself, and another one in the works. And in another few weeks she might even have a royalty check in the mail.

I don't need you, she whispered silently, catching sight of her grandfather as he stood, his face flushed, his thumbs hooked in the armholes of his vest, regaling an audience of neophyte lawyers with what a great, history-making man he was.

You're small, grandfather. Really, really small. Carson Beckett, a man I've known only two days, is twice the man you'll ever be.

Had it been only two days? Funny, she thought, in some ways it seemed as if she'd known him forever. The way her eyes kept constantly searching the crowded room, seeking him out, as if there were some invisible wire connecting them.

"I bought your little booklet, Katherine," said another friend of her grandmother, who had just joined the small group. "Naturally, I didn't read it, but I thought seeing that Flavia and I are close friends, I could at least do that much to support her only granddaughter."

Her little booklet. Kit wondered if the remark was intended to sound as condescending as it did. Giving the woman the benefit of doubt, she said, "Thank you, Mrs. Barnes. I appreciate that."

That booklet, as you call it, was nominated for an

award. It didn't get it, but it was mentioned in *Publishers Weekly.*

From some ten feet away, where he'd been trapped by an elderly bow-tied gentleman, Carson caught her eye and nodded toward the front door. The loquacious old gent remarked on the weather, offering the opinion that March would go out like a lamb. Edging away, Carson declined to comment on a certain candidate running for attorney general, explaining that he was from South Carolina. Then he laughed dutifully at the old saw about North Carolina being a vale of humility between two mountains of conceit—Virginia and his home state.

Once the old guy moved on, Carson considered his options. He could join Kit and meet her fawning gentleman friend, or he could wait for her at the front door.

He decided on the latter option, which took him close to the buffet where an array of finger food surrounded a five-tier wedding cake, the lower tier sporting enough candles to set off a sprinkler system. The sight of all that food reminded him that he hadn't eaten anything since the weed sandwich Kit had put together for lunch—hadn't even finished that, if he remembered correctly. On impulse, he picked up two plates and two forks and was just reaching for something brown wrapped in bacon when he heard his name called.

He turned to see Kit waving him over.

Yours to command, lady, he thought, replacing the plates and silverware. Funny thing—it would never have occurred to him to place her in a setting like this, yet she seemed perfectly at home here, godawful gorgeous dress and all.

Resigned to waiting at least five more minutes before he could politely make a break for it, he edged past another clump of partygoers and wondered what the devil was he doing here anyway—in the bosom, as it were, of her family. A Beckett and Chandler rematch?

No way.

He tried to regain his objectivity, knowing even as he did that it was a lost cause. Being objective around a woman like Kit Dixon was about like trying to ignore a swarm of ground bees.

And then he was there beside her, inhaling her unique scent among the Chanel and Polo and chicken livers.

Kit grabbed his wrist and pulled him closer. "Grandmother, this is Carson Beckett, an—an old friend." The look she shot him was pleading, the smile brittle and just a bit desperate. "Car, this is my grandmother, Mrs. Dixon, and this is Randolph Hart," the Ralph Fiennes look-alike. "Randolph is a friend of my grandfather's."

Carson shook hands with the man who was probably a year or two older, but with considerably less rough mileage on him.

"Beckett." Hart nodded.

The woman was older than he'd first thought, but extremely well preserved. Kit's grandmother favored him with a cool smile that never reached her eyes. For the next few minutes they engaged in polite, meaningless conversation. From habit, Carson summed up the other man as professional, successful, probably heterosexual. His posture indicated a certain proprietary interest in Kit, which she didn't seem to reciprocate.

Hmm.... A young lawyer and a judge's granddaughter?

Bingo, he thought a few minutes later as the old judge joined them. "I see you met Hart, here. Just been made a senior partner, d'he tell you that? Flavia, the Sawyers were asking about you, why don't you go over and talk to them." It was a command, not a request.

Flavia Dixon murmured something polite and left, the same fixed smile on her masklike face.

The judge turned then to Carson. "Randolph tell you about the party his folks are throwing to celebrate? He'll be taking my granddaughter, of course. Kit, see that you wear something more suitable, y'hear? Might make it a double celebration, right, son?"

The tone was jovial; the expression was not. The judge's cold gray eyes—Kit's eyes, but totally devoid of her warmth and sparkle—lingered on the flamboyant dress before moving to her hair, which had started out the evening gathered at the back of her neck by a big gold clasp. "Do something about that hair, too, while you're at it. Cut it off. Your grandmother can tell you where to go. God knows she spends enough of my money on herself."

"Grandfather, I'm afraid—" Kit's hand gripped Carson's arm. She edged closer, and he acted on impulse.

"What Kit's trying to say, sir, is she might not be available."

His flabby cheeks suddenly reddening, the judge glared at him, then turned to Kit. "What d'you mean, not available? You don't even know the date yet, so don't play your silly little games with me, girl."

Kit opened her mouth to speak, but Carson, covering her cold fingers with his own, took over. He might not know what was going on here, but he damned sure knew intimidation when he heard it. "What Kit means, sir, is that she's going home with me for a visit. We're not sure how long it will last, but my mother hasn't been well and she enjoys company. Then there's Lance and Liza, they live close by. You remember Kit's cousin Liza, don't you?"

He was damned sure the bastard didn't.

The old judge started to bluster, but cut it off. After

shooting a meaningful look at his protégé, he wheeled about and stalked off.

"You ready?" Carson asked, wanting to get her the hell away before anyone else tried to jerk her strings.

"Give me one minute."

While Kit made her way across the room to speak to her grandmother, Carson headed for the buffet again. Bypassing the stack of gold-rimmed china plates, he filched a couple of napkins and loaded them with finger food. The napkins were linen, which made it petty thievery, but what the hell. If food could help wipe away that stricken look on Kit's face, then he'd damn well feed her until she couldn't fit into that dress of hers.

After that, he would...

Don't go there, man. Don't even go there.

Eight

"I knew it would be bad," Kit said as soon as they were in the car, headed out the boxwood-lined circular driveway. "It always is, but—" She shook her head, then pressed two fingers to the pucker line between her eyebrows. "Why can't he ever learn? He's not stupid—far from it. It's the control thing, you know. He's just like my father was. It's always about control."

He wanted to ask about her parents, but knowing Kit, anything of importance would emerge soon enough if he let her ramble. He had learned through experience which tactics worked best on which personality types, even figuring in the fear factor. Which wasn't even a factor in this case. Trouble was, Kit wasn't a type, she was simply Kit, who didn't owe him any answers.

For several minutes the only sound was the whine of high-performance radials on damp pavement. Evidently there'd been a shower earlier. He thought about playing a CD as quiet, disarming background noise, but decided against it. She'd talk when she felt like talking, and if she didn't…

There was no law that said she had to talk to him.

"You cold?" he asked when the silence had stretched over several miles. Not that he was uncomfortable with silence, but this particular silence was too full of things that needed saying. On both sides.

When she didn't reply, he glanced over at her. She was shivering. The temperature had dropped at least ten degrees since they'd set out, probably when the showers passed through. Inside the car it was warm enough, though.

She took a deep breath and straightened up. "Cold? No, I'm fine. You do know what he's doing, don't you?"

It took him a minute to get up to speed. He ventured a guess. "Your grandfather?"

"He's matchmaking," she said grimly. "I ask you, does my grandfather strike you as the sentimental type?"

"Not particularly." A car passed on a long curve. Other than that, there was practically no traffic. "You think he's trying to pair you up with whatsisname? Hart?"

"More like engineering a merger, with him as the controlling partner," she responded bitterly. "He's not particularly subtle, is he?"

About as subtle as a sledgehammer. Carson watched the dark, flat countryside roll past and reduced his speed a few miles. "Wanna share?" he teased after several more minutes passed in silence. "You tell me yours and I'll tell you mine?"

Not that there was much to tell on his part. He had a feeling that what little there was was about to slip away, but that was another issue.

"Randolph—nobody's allowed to call him Randy since

he was made a partner in the firm—anyway, his father and my father were friends. Mr. Hart was on the same plane my parents were on when it crashed. You probably remember—it made headlines long enough a few years back. There was this big investigation and all sorts of rumors about a bomb or a missile. One theory was that there was this mob boss who was about to go on trial. My father was the prosecuting attorney, and some people thought they blew up the plane he was on to send a message.''

She shivered again, and Carson nudged the heat up a notch. It was either that or pull over and offer to share his body heat. Which just might present a distraction neither of them needed at this point.

After another long silence, she picked up the conversation where she'd left it. ''He thought he could take over after my father died, you know. Old Cast Iron, I mean. My grandfather.''

''Uh-huh,'' he said. A judge taking over his son's law practice?

''Not the firm—me.'' She answered the unvoiced question. ''He thought he could step in and take over my life, like I was one of his chess pieces. I was supposed to start by going to this fancy junior college—not for an education, you understand, but as sort of a holding tank until he figured out what he wanted to do with me next. Now, of course, he's got it all figured out, only I'm getting too old and he's royally ticked off.''

''Too old for what?''

''It has to do with my father's will. Oh, let's not get into that, it's too depressing.''

''Right.'' He waited to see if any more information would be forthcoming.

''Well.'' She adjusted her shoulder strap and said something about satin being so slippery. "I've never worn it before—at least not on the outside. I hate waste, though. I bought it on sale for an autograph session when my first book came out, but I ended up wearing clam-diggers and a Hawaiian print shirt. It was at Nags Head, you know. Good thing, too. I'd probably have slid right out of my chair. It was one of those folding metal ones, but they had a lovely flower arrangement with lollipops and daisies."

Evidently, the topic of wills and meddling grandfathers was closed. Carson shuffled the information into proper sequence and filled in a few gaps. He was getting used to her mode of expression, which was random, to put it mildly. Might be interesting to take a look at one of her books before he left, just to see if she rambled through a story the same way she rambled through everything else.

"Is that wind making the car rock like that? No wonder I'm freezing."

The breeze had picked up, but it wasn't particularly cold. "You're welcome to my jacket. Shirt, too, if you need it, but I'm not going to offer to change clothes with you. I have to tell you, purple's not my best color."

She laughed, which might have been the object of the whole inane exchange. "It's not purple, it's fuchsia." Then she sighed. "What a mess. Carson, I'm sorry as I can be I dragged you into it, but I really do appreciate your being there. I mean everything that's happened lately, not just the party. If I'd gone there alone tonight, I'd have walked out in a fit of temper and probably ended up getting arrested for speeding."

In the Ladybug? He doubted if she'd have been able to meet the minimum speed limit, but was tactful enough not to say so.

"And then, of course, someone would notify grandfather and he'd show up to bail me out and then he'd find

out about the rest of my mess and insist that I go back
home with him so he could ruin the rest of my life.''

Her mess. That was one way of putting it. ''I doubt if
you'd be jailed. I don't think the laws are that different
in North Carolina, but don't let that stop you if you're on
a roll.''

She sliced off a quick, sidelong grin that touched a
place that hadn't been touched in a long, long time—if
ever. ''Okay, so I exaggerate a little. It's my creative side.
I like to make a short story long and a dull story fancy.''

''Fancy?''

She shrugged again. It wasn't the first time he'd noticed
that about her—that she used her whole body and not just
her hands when she talked.

''Actually, except for a few minor details, I have my
life pretty much under control.''

''Right. Minor details like murder.'' Maybe he should
mention that a bit of grandfatherly interest at this point
might not be the worst thing that could happen to her. It
was not only her creative imagination that was making
her jumpy about this murder business. Like it or not, she
was a player.

She shivered again. She'd refused his coat the first time
he'd offered it. This time he didn't offer. Seeing a turnoff
just ahead, he pulled over and shut off the engine. She
looked startled, then wary. ''Is someone tailing us?'' she
whispered, glancing over her shoulder at the dark highway.

Carson eased his arms from the sleeves of his jacket.
''I'm getting hot—thought you might have changed your
mind about wearing it.''

Without waiting for an answer, he reached over and
draped it around her shoulders, then tugged her forward
and smoothed it down over her back. ''There, that ought

to do it," he muttered, jerking his hands away before they could get into trouble. Ever since he'd seen her preening in front of her bedroom mirror, holding that dress up in front of her, he'd been conscious of a growing sexual awareness. Suddenly, tension was snapping in the air like a live wire. Was he the only one affected? Once or twice tonight he'd caught her looking at him in a way that...

That was sheer wishful thinking on his part. There was nothing of a personal nature happening here—although sexual was not necessarily personal. On the other hand, with Kit, it would be.

Oh, yeah.

"What are you thinking?" she asked out of the blue.

"Nothing," he said, guilt and embarrassment making him feel like a raw kid. He'd known her for what—two days? He was no stranger to the occasional random attack of testosterone. But not with Kit. Whatever was between them was about to end, once he'd handed over the check—that damned check.

Besides, there was Margaret.

"You know what?" she said suddenly, squirming deeper into his coat like a kitten on a feather pillow. "I'm going to make some excuse to Jeff and just disappear until everything's settled. I hate to leave him shorthanded, but it's not like he's really rushed yet. Bambi can handle it."

She turned up the collar of his jacket, and without thinking, he reached out and lifted her hair outside. It was warm and alive. Her faint fruity scent eddied around him, and he thought, I gotta get out of here, I'm flat-out losing it.

As if totally oblivious to the meltdown taking place in the seat beside her, Kit said thoughtfully, "I'm pretty sure I can finish the illustrations from memory. I've already done the sketches and value studies. I can look around for another job and a place to stay. I really like Gil's Point, but you know what? I think something—or someone, is trying to tell me it's time to move on." After a moment she added, "I believe in fate, I really do."

She believed in *fate?*

When it came to the *F* word, Carson believed in family, food and fishing, in that order. Fate was not something he'd spent a whole lot of time pondering.

"I have a better idea," he heard himself saying. "Why not come home with me, like we told your grandfather?"

Jesus. Where did that come from?

"Oh, I couldn't," she said, but he could tell it was a halfhearted protest.

Before his brain could cut in, he dug himself in even deeper. "I wasn't lying when I said my mother loves company. I have to warn you, though—she might not even recognize me. She's in the early stages of Alzheimer's."

Without waiting for a response to his impulsive invitation, he switched on the engine and shifted into Reverse. Both his hands were occupied, so this time instead of touching his arm, she laid her hand on his thigh. Same cold fingers; same electrifying grip. Margaret wasn't a toucher. His mother was, and so was his Aunt Becky.

Kit's touch was in a whole different category.

"Carson, I'm so sorry. You certainly don't have to follow through just because of what you told my grandfather. I've been on my own for seven years, and I've managed just fine. I drive hundreds of miles, looking for story locations—you see, I have to be able to visualize things—I mean, even before I start writing, I need to know where a story will take place. What I'm trying to say is, I know lots of places to go if I want to disappear for a while."

"Sure you do," he said, pulling out onto the highway. They were no more than fifteen or twenty minutes from

Gil's Point. "Still, why not humor me? See, I have this personal problem…"

He toyed with the idea of telling her about his mother's fixation on weddings and Margaret, his "sort-of" fiancée, who'd been taking a few too many trips to New York lately. Before he could decide, she leaned forward and peered through the windshield.

"What's that glow up ahead? Look—over there." They were approaching the bridge at Coinjock over the inland waterway. To the north, about where Gilbert's Point would be located, the night sky was suspiciously red.

"Wrong season for the Northern Lights," he murmured. "Brush fire reflected on low clouds?" He had a funny feeling it was something far different. The only thing he'd seen in that general direction was water, marsh and a few wooded knolls. Nothing to support a sustained fire.

By the time they topped the bridge, the location was no longer a mystery. The brightness had diminished to a sullen glow, and it was definitely centered in the vicinity of Gilbert's Point.

"Oh, God, not the Crab House," Kit murmured. "They've been on him about that exhaust fan…."

Carson didn't bother to ask who "they" were. It wasn't the restaurant, or anything else along the waterfront. By the time they'd reached the tiny waterfront settlement, the source of the glow was all too evident. Creeping along through the huddled spectators and emergency vehicles, Carson pulled up beside the abandoned house that stood a few hundred feet away from what remained of Kit's rental house.

She hadn't said a word, but he could hear her shuddering breath. Feeling a degree of rage that was surprising, considering the kinds of cases he'd been working on for the past few years, he swore silently. She didn't need this, not on top of everything else. A total loss—the house, everything in it—even her car.

They'd left the Ladybug parked in its usual place, beside a lone section of picket fence. The fence was down, either burned or trampled by the emergency crews. They were all there—firemen, deputies, EMTs—an ambulance was pulled over to one side.

Silently, he surveyed the crowd before turning his attention back to the ruins. The fire was mostly out by now, only a few hot spots flaring up. The only thing left standing was a chimney, the plumbing and the refrigerator.

He turned to Kit, an irreverent crack on the tip of his tongue. Stress occasionally brought out that sort of thing among cops. Sometimes the tension needed just releasing.

Whatever he'd been going to say went unsaid.

Staring straight ahead, she was about as still as a body could be and still breathe. As if sensing his gaze on her, she turned to him, her eyes dark with pain. With shock. "I had an appointment to get the transmission repaired," she said with quiet dignity.

Carson unsnapped his seat belt, then reached over and unclipped hers. And then he did what he'd been wanting to do all evening, but for entirely different reasons—or maybe not.

He hauled her into his arms. "Shh, we'll take care of it," he murmured. He'd buy her another car. Hell, he'd buy her a fleet of the things if it made her happy, he thought irrationally.

She didn't say a word, just burrowed into his warmth, her fists working their way up under his arms like a pair of heat-seeking missiles.

If she wanted heat...

Not now, dammit!

Holding her, feeling the small shudders that coursed through her body, Carson heard himself making the kind of ineffectual sounds that were meant to comfort. Meanwhile, his mind was racing along three separate tracks at once.

Had to be arson, but why? Insurance? He could easily find out who owned the place, but the timing was too pat.

A warning?

Or something more serious. A calm sort of resolution came over him. Let the locals figure out what it was all about—that was their job. His was getting her the hell away from here.

She wasn't crying, at least he didn't think she was. He almost wished she would. Evidently the pressure had been building since before he'd ever met her. Before she'd practically knocked him off his feet.

His arms tightened. He moved his hands up and down her back, his palms sliding over the slick fabric under his own jacket. When his fingers felt the band of her bra, his imagination took off on a course of its own before he could rein it in.

Back off, man, you're way out of line!

What was it with this woman? It had to be some bizarre chemical reaction that triggered a hormone attack every time he touched her—or even thought about touching her. He reminded himself for the second time in less than an hour that he was too old for this kind of thing. Not *old*-old, just too old for Kit, he amended quickly.

Forcing his mind away from the woman in his arms—the woman who was clinging to him, her arms around his waist, her knee poking into his hip and her head burrowed under his jaw, Carson directed his attention to the scene in front of him. The situation warranted his full attention, because something dirty was going on here.

As if sensing his change of focus, Kit took a deep breath and pulled away. Together they stared at the half-dozen volunteer firemen watering down the ruins. Not that there was anything left to save. The fire had burned too hot, too fast. Carson had to wonder if she'd had any sense of precognition when she'd mentioned the refrigerator as a safe place in case the house caught fire. Good thing he hadn't taken her at her word.

She finally spoke, her voice low, but steadier than he would have expected. "I didn't know—I never dreamed—I'm so sorry about your check. I guess if something, even a refrigerator gets hot enough, anything in it might get scorched."

"Scorched. Yeah, that about describes it." His mind was busy gathering and collating impressions. "It was your check, not mine. And in case you were worried, it's in my briefcase in the back seat. I didn't leave it."

He'd seen the blackened refrigerator and thought about her earlier suggestion that she leave it there in case the house caught fire. Along with being psychic, was she also a mind reader? Somehow, it wouldn't surprise him. He only hoped she didn't pick up on the way his body reacted to the scent of her, the feel of her—hell, even the sight of her in her crazy, wild-colored clothes.

"My poor car," she whispered.

"I'm really sorry about that, honey. I know it meant a lot to you." The endearment just slipped out. In his family, it was a comfort word. As in, *"Have another piece of chicken, honey, you need to build up your strength."*

"It needed a new transmission, did I tell you? And some other parts, too," she said wistfully. "I made an appointment for next week. I can't really afford it yet—royalties won't be out until May, and they're not all that much. But I have to have my car in case I want to—to move or something.''

When her voice squeaked and broke it was all he could do not to drag her back into his arms and promise to buy her the car of her dreams. The woman was obviously screwing up his mind on more than one level.

He started to tell her that with ten thousand dollars to spend, she could easily afford a new transmission, but under the circumstances, it might be better not to mention it. ''Look, I need to speak to the firemen, but—''

But I hate to leave you here alone, he finished silently. Fortunately, he had sense enough not to say it. Fragility mixed with independence and impulsiveness was a dangerous combination.

Someone rapped on the window and he turned away. Seeing a familiar face, he rolled down the glass, but didn't speak. His look said it all.

''Man, this is rough,'' Jeff said. ''When we saw Kit's car, we thought—'' The Crab House proprietor broke off, obviously shaken. Leaning down, he looked past Carson and said, ''Thank God you were gone, Kit. Look, I've got a spare room I can clean out if you need a place to stay, and Bambi—she's right over there—'' He indicated the cluster of onlookers still huddled behind one of the bright yellow fire trucks, ''She says she can put you up if you don't mind sleeping double.''

''Thanks Jeff, but—''

Carson took over. ''She appreciates it, but she's going home with me. Sorry about leaving you in the lurch like this, but under the circumstances…'' He didn't elaborate. Didn't need to. The guy was sharper than he looked, and he was obviously deeply concerned.

Jeff nodded and straightened up, but left both red-knuckled hands on the door. ''Hey, we can handle things okay at the restaurant. Bambi's got a friend that can fill in if we get in a bind, so you go ahead—do whatever you need to do. Too much going down around here lately anyhow, if you ask me.''

"You got that right," Carson muttered. "Hang around a minute, will you, Matlock? I want to go speak to one of the firefighters.''

Carson left after telling Kit he'd be back in three minutes. After surveying the scene, he homed in on one of the firemen in full turnout gear. He needed certain suspicions confirmed. If these guys were as sharp as they appeared, they could tell him what he needed to know without waiting for lab results.

And then he'd get her to hell out of this place, the sooner, the better.

Nine

Less than twenty minutes later they were on their way, Carson's worst fears confirmed. The deputy sheriff had dismissed his questions about the cause of the fire, even though the smell of gasoline still hung in the air, mingled with the acrid smell of smoke.

"Nah, these old houses, they go up this way all the time," the young law officer had replied. "Wiring shoulda been inspected, but you can't get these locals to do a damned thing."

These locals? Who did the little jerk think he was working for? Carson had seen similar cases, when some kid fresh out of training pinned on a little too much attitude along with his badge.

"Funny, it doesn't smell like an electrical fire," Carson had observed. He didn't know what an electrical fire would smell like when the house had burned to the ground, but he'd lay odds that it didn't smell like gasoline.

The deputy had abruptly wheeled away to bark orders to a bystander who wandered too close while Carson lingered a few more minutes, looking for something that would deflect his suspicions. Lightning, for instance.

But if there'd been a lightning storm, someone would have mentioned it. And lightning didn't smell like gasoline. According to the volunteer firemen he'd spoken with, no effort had been made to disguise the agent used. "Don't know if there was any insurance or not. These old places..." He shook his head, his meaning clear. Houses this old weren't worth insuring, especially if they contained a woodstove or a working fireplace.

Carson had brought up the fact that the VW had been far enough from the house so that it shouldn't have ignited on its own.

"Gas tank coulda had a leak. Might've flashed over. Shame, though. I wouldn't mind owning it, myself. Old times sake, y'know. Used to have one, but mine was gray. Coulda painted it up like a moth, I reckon, if I'da thought about it." He shook his head, and Carson left him to his job of wetting down the surroundings and any flare-ups.

Whether or not the car had burned was not as important as what its presence outside the house indicated. This time of night, whoever had poured gasoline around all four sides of the house and tossed a match had to have considered the possibility—hell, the probability—that Kit was inside. That thought alone chilled him right down to the marrow.

Ruling out insurance fraud and accident, one question remained. Had the fire been intended to scare a witness into silence?

Or to silence her permanently?

Fortunately, she hadn't asked questions when he'd come back to the car. The locals had their work cut out for them, but with a few notable exceptions, they were probably up to handling it. Not all the brains were found in the big city. Some of the county offices he'd had dealings with could be every bit as effective. They always had access to the SBI—and in this case, possibly the DEA.

Back at the car, he exchanged places with Jeff Matlock. "Thanks, I'll take over now. We'll be in touch in a day or so."

His instincts told him the guy was trustworthy, and until this case was wrapped up he was going to need a contact here, someone who was on the site, someone who knew who belonged in the neighborhood and who didn't. Because no matter how long it took, Carson wasn't about to bring her back here until this business was wrapped up with no loose ends left to trip over.

Legally, any dwelling could be considered inhabited whether or not it was actually occupied at the time of a fire. Getting rid of the gunshot victim had indicated a certain level of professionalism, but in this case, the job had been crudely and quickly done, with little attempt to make it look like an accident. Either the perp was an idiot, or he was desperate. Either way, Carson wanted Kit out of there.

They were on the way out Waterlily Road when Kit spoke for the first time since they'd driven away from the scene. She was wearing his sport coat over her dress, but with her arms wrapped around her body, she still looked cold. She was quiet, too. With Kit, that was a cause for concern, because she was a talker. Carson made a mental note to watch for signs of shock.

"Do you think I should call the sheriff again and tell him what we know?" she asked.

"Your call, but think about it first. You heard an argument, you heard a shot, you saw a body, right? You've already reported all that.''

''I know.'' She sighed, her hands now clasped between her knees.

Nearing the intersection with Highway 158, he rolled to a stop. One look in those wide gray eyes of hers and he wanted to pull over, take her in his arms and hold her until some of the sense of unreality she must be feeling went away. Something like this was all in a day's work for him, but not for Kit.

Not for any civilian, but Kit in particular. She was too much like one of the fairytale creatures in her own stories—not that he'd actually read one, but he'd seen the covers, marveling that this woman—this flaky creature who had tried to run him down, and who showed no interest in the money he kept trying to give her, had actually created those images.

She wasn't crying. He would have expected her to be crying by now. Hell, she was homeless. She'd lost everything but that wildly impractical dress and those sexy, accident-waiting-to-happen shoes.

Funny thing about crying, he mused as the miles rolled past in silence. Kids cried when they were physically hurt—sometimes when they were scared. Adults didn't. He'd seen women endure unbelievable pain without shedding a single tear. Emotional injuries, though....

When did it change? Was it part of the rite of puberty? No more crying over ouchies now, you're an adult. Cry when your heart's breaking—curse when anything else gets broken.

Crying or not, she needed holding. He wanted to hold her, too, but he didn't dare, not now. She was so brittle it wouldn't take much to break her, and until he could get some answers, he needed her whole and functioning.

He'd figure out where they were going later.

She spoke after half an hour of silence, in answer to God only knows which question. "It just seems...I don't know. Fishy," she said thoughtfully.

Fishy? His mind raced back over the past half hour, trying to connect the dots. Trying to connect anything.

"Well, think about it. I report finding a body, the body disappears, and then it's found again. It has to be the same one, don't you think? I mean, Gil's Point is just too small for two bodies in as many days."

He nodded slowly as a few dots connected.

She continued. "And then, right after all that, my house burns to the ground." She looked at him then, her face too pale, her features too finely drawn. Shocky, but hanging in there. "You know what I think? I think someone deliberately set that fire to hurt me."

Smart lady. "We can't be certain if that's true. On the other hand, it doesn't hurt to think defensively until we find out a few facts."

"You're a policeman. What would you do if you were me?"

By then they had turned off onto Highway 158, headed generally west. He was a cop; she had that much right. But even on his own turf it wasn't always possible to walk the line without stepping in something sticky. In a case like this, where he was clearly out of his jurisdiction, he was operating at a slight disadvantage. Better to work from a safe distance. If she checked in again with the local law and tried to tell her story—and knowing the way Kit's mind worked, it would involve a few embellishments— she might end up being held as a material witness. Especially if that young jerk deputy had anything to do with it. He was a little too impressed with his shiny new badge and that big .45 strapped to his porcine hip.

Carson made a mental note to run an unofficial check on the county law office. Until then, he wanted her out of range.

"Citizens have a duty," Kit said out of the blue, and then seemed to lose her chain of thought.

"Look, you followed the unwritten rules." He tried to sound reassuring.

"I don't know any unwritten rules."

"That's because they're not written down anywhere." With one hand on the wheel, he reached for a body part to comfort, found her thigh, and patted. "Rule number one, you move away from what's going down. Don't get involved. You pegged that one, right?"

"Hmm." A sidelong glance revealed her face in the faint glow of the dashboard. She was looking only slightly more relaxed. Maybe his tactics were working.

"Okay, next you notify the proper authorities, report only what you saw or heard—no more, no less—and you do it promptly." To the best of his knowledge, she had complied to the letter.

She drew in a shuddering breath.

"I can turn up the heat," he suggested. It was North Carolina, not North Dakota. It was March, for Pete's sake. They were already a day or two into spring.

Suddenly she leaned forward and said, "Slow down." They were nearing the turnoff that would take them to Highway 17. "See that service station up ahead? That's where one of the deputies lives—the newest one. I don't know his name—I don't even know what he looks like. He could've been one of the men there tonight—at the house, I mean."

Where the house used to be, Carson corrected, but had the good sense to do it silently.

"Anyway, when I wanted to rent the house on the other

side—the little brick bungalow? The rental agent said he'd just leased it to a new deputy sheriff."

Fortunately, traffic was light, otherwise he might get hauled over as a navigational hazard. Carson slowed down and studied the place, reluctant to stop for no real reason other than the instinctive need he felt to get her away from there. "Guy's probably still at the fire."

"Did you see any deputies there?"

"A couple." Neither of them, including the jerk with the attitude, had looked old enough to shave, but then, that might be his own personal bias. He didn't need the reminder that Kit was closer to their ages than to his. "Seen enough?"

"Wait, there's a light on," she said, bracing herself on his thigh to see past him. The house in question was on the left. There was a big fig tree close to the highway that partially blocked the view. "Maybe I should just…"

The security light from the service station spilled over onto the yard. Ignoring a nagging sense of reluctance, he was about to pull into the driveway when he heard her gasp. The fingers on his thigh dug in. "Go, go go!" she whispered fiercely. "Don't stop!"

What the devil—?

After a swift glance into the rearview mirror, he veered back onto the highway. Fortunately, the only headlights in sight were a safe distance behind, but something had sure as hell spooked her.

"You want to tell me what's going on here?" As a rule he was pretty much a by-the-book man. Saved time and trouble in the long run. But ever since she'd nearly run him down, he'd been operating on instinct, and now even that was going haywire. Like trying to steer his way through an iron foundry using an old fashioned compass.

He had a feeling he knew what to blame, too. Didn't

want to know. Couldn't afford to think about it. He'd sooner rack it up to a side effect of the twenty-four-hour virus that had caught up with him in Nags Head and followed him to Gilbert's Point.

But this particular symptom had little to do with the flu and even less to do with a possible drug-related murder. It had everything to do with the woman beside him, her short, unpolished fingernails digging into the muscles of his thigh.

Did she even know she still had her hand there? She couldn't possibly know how it was affecting him—how everything about her affected him.

Hell, it didn't make sense.

He revved up to five miles above the limit, keeping an eye on the rearview mirror while he did his best to ignore the steely grip that was digging in mere inches from ground zero. When he was pretty sure he could speak calmly, he said, "You want to tell me what just happened back there?"

She removed her hand, raked it through her hair and took a deep breath, turning to face forward again. "That truck. Carson, it's the same one."

He waited. *Details at eleven, folks.*

She unclipped her seat belt, twisted around and came up on her knees to stare at the scene fast falling behind. When she braced herself with one hand on his shoulder, he reached down and angled a vent to blow on his face. He was sweating. If he'd thought a vehicle this size could safely hold two adults without either of them infringing on the other's personal space, he'd thought wrong. This woman could be at the opposite end of the damned county and she'd still manage to mess up his concentration.

And if that made any sense, he'd eat his boots. Minus catsup.

Finally she turned around and settled back into her seat. He growled, "Fasten your seat belt. Don't do that again, all right?"

Dutifully, she sat down again and clicked the buckle. He shot her a suspicious look. "You want to tell me what it was all about?"

"I told you. Weren't you even listening?"

"You didn't tell me one damned thing, you just yelled, go, go, go!"

"I did so tell you." She sounded affronted.

Which, he reluctantly conceded, was better than sounding terrified. A whole lot better. "So tell me again, I'm a little slow on the uptake."

"I know, you've been sick and then you got all mixed up in my—my—" She tugged at her seat belt to loosen it. "I'm sorry as I can be that I got you involved, but that truck back there—Carson, it's the same one. You know, the man who was messing around with Ladybug when I thought he was planting explosives? And I yelled at him and he ran?"

He knew about a truck. At least, he remembered hearing her disjointed account of what had happened when she'd gone to retrieve her car the first time. He never lost details, but sometimes when data came piling in too rapidly, he simply crammed it into a mental heap to sort out later.

They were on a narrow straight stretch of highway through wide-open farmland. Carson pulled off onto the shoulder beside a newly planted field. "Listen, before we go any further, I want you to tell me everything you know."

She swallowed audibly. "Everything?"

"No frills, just the facts, ma'am." He waited, but she was evidently too young to remember Sergeant Friday on the old cop show. "You said the guy who was messing around with your car drove off in a pickup." He'd been a bit feverish at the time, his head threatening implosion, but he did remember that much.

"It was the same one. I was already scared, so I noticed. It was red, with one blue fender, like he'd had to replace it or something. And the sound it made—remember I told you about the truck at the church? Vroom, vroom, and then this funny whine?"

Details began slotting into place. He nodded.

"Well, I knew I'd heard it before when I heard it again, and I'm sure it was the same truck, even if I didn't see the license plate. But of course, I didn't see it the first time, either, so that didn't matter. I can't actually swear on a stack of Bibles that it was the same truck that was in the church parking lot, but Carson—you know what I'm thinking?"

He knew what *he* was thinking. Unfortunately—not to mention inappropriately—it had nothing to do with pickup trucks, with or without blue fenders and muffler packs. He marked it down to a heightened stress level on top of a long, dry spell, sexually speaking. For good measure he threw in that provocative scent she was wearing. Fruity, spicy, with overtones of smoke.

She was shivering again. If he turned the heat up any more, he'd have to shed some clothes. Under the circumstances, that wasn't advisable. Middle of the night—shut up together in close confines, heightened emotions—it was a conflagration waiting to happen.

He was three years shy of forty, for crying out loud, not seventeen! Evidently that concussion he'd sustained five months ago had done more damage than he'd thought.

"Look, we never did eat lunch, and I don't know about

you, but I didn't get anything to eat at your folks' party.
You want to find a drive-in and fill up?''

On any other woman, the look she shot him could have
been called indignant. On Kit, it was...

Simply Kit. A unique woman with a unique set of problems. Problems he seemed to have taken onto his own
shoulders.

They drove for several miles before finding food that
didn't come out of a vending machine. By the time he
pulled up to the gas tanks, Carson had remembered the
napkins full of party food he'd tossed onto the back seat.
Whatever that was wrapped in bacon—chicken livers,
probably—he figured it wasn't worth the risk. Besides, he
needed to fill his gas tank, and they could both use the
facilities. Too much had happened since he'd showered,
shaved and set out to attend an anniversary celebration at
a fancy estate on the Chesapeake Bay.

Kit hurried inside, teetering on those ridiculous shoes.
He filled his tank, then went inside. Before heading to the
men's room, he placed an order for two Italian subs on
whole wheat, with everything, reasoning that any woman
who ate weeds would probably go for whole grain bread.

His face, the collar of his shirt and the edges of his hair
still damp, he was just putting away his billfold a few
minutes later when she emerged from the ladies' room,
looking so pale her freckles stood out in relief.

And so damned appealing it was all he could do not to
open his arms. How was it possible for a woman to look
that good wearing an ugly dress, a man's coat that was
about six sizes too large, and hair had evidently been
groomed by a hay-rake?

Those shoes would have to go, he thought, watching
her make her way past the popcorn and potato chips. Even
exhausted and stressed out, she had an in-your-face way

of walking that was sexy as the devil. *Here I come, world, get the hell out of my way.*

Only she didn't curse. He'd noticed that about her, along with a few thousand more details.

"Want your coat back?" she asked, eyeing the thick six-inch subs that were just being wrapped.

"Keep it. I'd lend you my boots, but they're probably half a size too big."

"Ha. Try five sizes too big."

She was game, all right. Strung out like a thread of molten glass and about as brittle, but she was hanging in there. He said, "Did you know you toe out when you walk?" *Trivial Pursuit* had its purposes.

"It's the shoes. I have to scrunch my toes to keep them on."

"We're going shopping first chance we get."

"You forget, I don't have—"

The clerk was eyeing them as if they might be from another planet. Or maybe he was eyeballing Kit, who was definitely worth the effort. "Let's go." He cut her off before she could remind him that she didn't have any money. Hell, he knew that. She had ten grand, but it wouldn't do her much good until she could get to a bank. Even then she might have trouble. He didn't know how much identification she had in that postcard-sized purse she'd carried with her to Virginia, but he had an idea it might not be sufficient.

All the more reason to take her home with him.

He ushered her out the door, thinking, okay, Beckett, what are you going to do with her once you get her to Charleston? Show up on your mama's doorstep with a stranger in tow? He'd spoken impulsively at the party, thinking to give her an easy out. It wasn't like him to do anything impulsively. He was a plodding, by-the-book kind of guy, for the most part.

Even so, it might have worked just fine a year ago, but not now. Things were shaky enough around there without adding someone like Kit Dixon to the equation.

What now? Find a hotel near a shopping mall, pay for a week's rent and lend her his charge card? The only other option he could think of was taking her home with him. To his two-bedroom, semi-furnished house outside Charleston proper.

"My feet hurt. I wish I'd worn my sneakers tonight instead of these things."

"We'll look for one of those 24/7 places that sells everything from truck tires to lady's lingerie."

She nodded, unwrapping her sub. "Thank you. I always wear sensible shoes—well, usually. You might not believe me, but I'm actually a very sensible person."

Surprisingly enough, without a scrap of evidence, he did believe her. Kit's notion of sensible might not agree with his, but she had walked away from security and made a life for herself. A successful life, considering she was a published author.

She took a big bite, closed her eyes and chewed. "Just what I needed," she said when she could speak again. "I don't have a toothbrush or a hairbrush, either. Or toothpaste or deodorant. Maybe I'd better make a list."

"Eat first." He'd pulled over into a space near the back of the lot, away from the brightest lights. Not that he wasn't capable of multitasking, but not driving and eating—when he was already distracted.

What was his family going to make of her? he wondered. "If you don't like hot peppers, take 'em out," he said.

"Love 'em." She took a bite of sandwich and reached for the milk he'd bought to put out the fire.

What was she going to make of his family?

And why did it matter?

He didn't know the answer, he only knew it mattered.

Ten

Kit took another bite of her sandwich, then carefully wrapped the remainder and placed it on the dashboard just as lightning flickered across the sky. She counted off the seconds, waiting for the sound of thunder, then yawned and said, "Ten miles. Maybe twelve, I count fast. The book I was working on? It's gone, you know. All three drafts and all the sketches I'd done." Her voice threatened to break, but steadied. "And my other books. There were only two, but I had a full shelf of authors' copies of each one. The first one's not even in print any longer." She took a deep breath. "Oh, well—I can probably find a few copies in a secondhand bookstore once I get settled again and have time to search." She flashed him a smile that was too quick, too brittle and faded far too soon.

"Don't you have a backup?"

"You mean like on a computer?" She shook her head. "I don't use a computer, I write in longhand and then hire the last draft typed. My stories aren't really long enough to require word processing.'' The truth was, she'd started out using a computer, but when the hard drive crashed, she couldn't afford to replace it. With only the outlay for legal pads and pencils, she could easily afford to hire the last draft typed. Any excess funds she accumulated could better be spent on art materials.

Carson started to speak, and she shook her head. ''I know, everyone uses the things, but just let me touch a keyboard and all sorts of weird things start happening. Messages pop out of nowhere. Stupid icons I don't understand hop all over the screen and this wicked genie flashes a red error message telling me I've committed some criminal offence and the computer police are already on the way to arrest me.''

He chuckled as if he knew exactly what she was talking about. Maybe he did. Men's brains were different from women's. ''I'm okay with computers,'' he said. ''Mechanical stuff, though—not too swift there.''

''Well, as long as we're comparing inadequacies, I can't even program my clock radio without having it go off in the middle of the night. Give me a simple, logical set of instructions and I do just fine.'' If she bothered to read the instructions, that was. Usually, she didn't. Not enough plot to waste her good reading time on.

More lightning flashed in the southwest, followed by a long rumble of thunder. Rain, Kit told herself, might put out the rest of the fire but it was far too late to do her poor old house any good.

Carson reached over and covered her hand with his, as if he knew what she was thinking. He couldn't possibly understand, but along with all the other things he was— which she couldn't afford to think about right now—he was kind and caring. Far more than most men she knew. Even Jeff had his limits.

"It's not the clothes I mind so much, or the things I bought for the house," she said after several minutes passed in silence. "All that can be replaced. But my work—" Breaking off, she took several deep breaths. "I took a course in jewelry making once at the community college. I wanted to make a pair of earrings, only when I got the first one done, I couldn't bring myself to make the other one. Been there, done that—you know what they say. I should've started out with a pin or a ring." She tried to laugh at her own shortcomings. Pinch-pleating her skirt between thumb and fingers, she said, "What I'm trying to explain is why I can't just pull a full-blown story out of my mind, even one I've already written. It's like my brain has lots of little doors and if I try to open the same door twice, it says, you've already been there, and it won't open and let me in again. Does that make any sense at all? And the drawings..."

For a long time Carson didn't say anything, and she thought, men couldn't understand. Then she changed it to people who aren't writers couldn't understand. Actually, Carson had been surprisingly understanding. Surprisingly supportive. She wasn't used to that—to having someone other than herself to depend on.

"I don't even know where we're going," she said with the closest thing to a smile she could manage. "If you're planning to take me to my grandparents' home again, I'd just as soon you let me out here. I'll call someone. There's a phone booth right over there."

"Call who, Matlock?"

"Mmm-hmm," she said, knowing she wouldn't. Jeff would come for her in a minute, but she didn't want to be beholden to him. Didn't want to be beholden to anyone, including Carson Beckett. Independence was too hard to establish, too tough to maintain, to risk blowing it on account of a single setback.

So then, why was she here?

Because. It was the only answer she could come up with that didn't scare the bejabbers out of her, and she'd been scared enough for one day.

She yawned, and then did it again. "Is that clock right?"

"Two minutes fast." His voice sounded gruff, but it was a good kind of gruff. Not angry. She couldn't have handled anger, not now. "I'm so sleepy I feel like I could hibernate for a solid year. Could we maybe just stay here and doze for—" she yawned "—half an hour?"

"I've got a better idea." Carson laid aside his unfinished sub and started the engine. He didn't feel sorry for her, he told himself. Well, he did, but that wasn't what bothered him most. Kit—no, damn it, Kit *Dixon!* Why did he keep thinking of her as Kit Carson? And what was the implication of pairing their two first names? Just because once upon a time there was a cowboy...

The woman easily fit the description of a walking disaster. With a layer of makeup and about a yard whacked off that skirt, she could pass for a streetwalker. Give her a turban and a few more pounds of jewelry and she could pass for a gypsy fortune-teller.

Funny thing, though, in spite of what that guy at Nags Head had said about living with her—in spite of everything—he had a feeling she was pretty inexperienced. Which was one more reason to take her somewhere safe, hand over the money and leave her the hell alone.

Because he was entirely too interested, and for all the wrong reasons.

He cleared his throat and said, "We both need a good

night's sleep. We can figure out the next step tomorrow with clearer heads.''

His next step would be toward Charleston. Hers would be…up to her. He might suggest that she go back to her grandfather and let him help her get copies of whatever papers she'd lost in the fire. Then she could cash the check and head out again. Start a new story—do whatever it was that writers of children's books did.

But jeez, it had to be rough, losing her books like that. Even worse than losing her social security card and whatever records she kept, because records could be duplicated. He knew how he'd felt when some creep had stolen his favorite spinning rod and a lifetime collection of tackle, including at least fifty hand-tied flies his father had made back before his arthritis had gotten too bad.

Carson pulled back out onto the highway, leaving the brightly lit, all-but-deserted station behind. What he needed more than anything was to put a few miles between them so that he could regain his perspective.

Yeah, like that was even a remote possibility.

Kit opened her eyes when they stopped again. They were parked outside a neat roadside motel. She couldn't recall ever seeing it before, which meant they weren't anywhere near her grandfather's house.

Carson said, ''Wait here, I'll get us a couple of rooms.''

''I don't have any luggage.''

''Neither do I,'' he said dryly, reminding her that his overnight bag had been in the house when it had burned.

Oh, great. Just what she needed—one more layer of guilt stacked up on top of everything else. Not only had she knocked him into a ditch and then embroiled him in her messy life, now she'd gone and destroyed his clothes.

''Honey, these people aren't exactly morality police.''

"I didn't mean that," she said quickly, but of course, she had. Just that morning she had woken up with the comforting feeling of not being alone. For a moment it had felt so good. So right.

"Be back in a minute."

When he turned to leave, she called him back. Closing her eyes, she blurted, "Carson—could you ask if they have, uh—rooms with two beds?"

After a long silence during which she wanted to tie herself to a railroad track or something equally melodramatic, he said, "That would be called a double room, right? I'll ask."

She watched him walk away—limp away, actually, although even with a slight limp, he had a macho walk. Not a swagger, they were both far too exhausted to swagger, but more like a jaguar than a bunny rabbit. That was the closest she could come, picturing him in one of her stories as a big, ferocious-looking cat. With a heart of gold, of course.

Oh, God, woman, you are so pathetic!

She looked grungy. She smelled like smoke. Everything smelled like smoke, like one of those underground peat fires that burned for years in the Dismal Swamp area. Her beautiful dress that she'd never even worn before tonight smelled like smoke with a hint of vinegar from the sub that had leaked in her lap. She didn't even know if the fabric was washable. Not that it mattered now. After tonight she never wanted to see the thing again.

The fact that he was still limping only added to her burden of guilt. Watching through the plate-glass window as he crossed the lobby, she had to remind herself that he was a stranger. A stranger dressed in western-style boots all mucked up now with wet ashes and mud, his khakis stained with soot and his blue shirt, several shades paler than his cobalt eyes, rumpled and probably soot-stained, too. His hair needed combing, his jaw needed shaving, and he walked as if it hurt to move.

Darn it, a man like that had no business being so blasted sexy!

And she had no business noticing. Her whole world was falling apart, and all she could think of was what it would be like to lie in the arms of a certain stranger and forget everything that had happened. Forget the argument, the gunshot and that poor man they'd brought in from Martha's Creek.

Forget her grandfather, who was determined to draw her back in the fold, not because he loved her but because he wanted to control her. Or at least to control the money her father had left her in the will he'd never gotten around to changing before he died. Even now the power struggle between the two men continued.

Dear Lord, Grandmother, couldn't you for once in your life stand up for me?

But then, why wish for miracles? Flavia Dixon was as much under that cast-iron thumb as her son and daughter-in-law had ever been. As Randolph Hart, her grandfather's handpicked candidate for the Katherine stakes, was now.

As Kit herself never had been and never would be.

"You're sure about the double room? They've got several singles. I can easily change it." Carson slid in under the steering wheel, but didn't shut the door.

She was tempted to change her mind, but didn't, because she'd already put him to so much trouble. But for her, he'd already be on his way back to Charleston.

But for her, he would never have left there.

"Do you mind? I don't snore—at least, I don't think I do."

"Snore away, I'm too bushed to notice anything short of a freight train passing through the room."

Inside the pleasant, impersonal room, Kit looked at the pair of queen-sized beds, then at the open bathroom door. She'd give her next royalty check for a toothbrush and a clean nightgown, or at least an oversized T-shirt.

As if reading her mind, Carson spoke up. "If you don't mind a T-shirt that that's been worn a few hours, you can have mine. Might be more comfortable than sleeping in your, um—skivvies.

"How about you?"

He shot her one of the quirky grins she'd seen too few of lately. As tired as she was, it was still powerful enough to register in places no smile was supposed to register.

"Boxers," he said. "D'you mind?"

"I'm the one who asked you to share, remember? Rooms, I mean—not underwear. I always hated being alone in the dark." Especially the times she'd been confined for some real or imagined offense to a dark closet for hours on end. "I always leave a small light on somewhere in the house. At least I did," she added, the afterthought bringing a sharp stab of regret.

"We'll leave the bathroom light on with the door partly closed. Go grab the first shower, I'll reach in and hang my T-shirt on the inside doorknob."

Carson listened for the sound of the shower, then peeled off his shirt, stripped off his undershirt and hung it where she could reach it, just inside the bathroom. Then he shrugged on his blue Brooks Brothers shirt again, leaving it unbuttoned, and stretched out across one of the two beds.

No way was he going to undress until she was sawing logs. The thought of spending the next few hours only a few feet apart, sharing a set of his underwear between them, was enough to short-circuit any common sense he had ever possessed.

His thoughts moved restlessly between Gilbert's Point and Charleston. First thing in the morning he needed to check in and see how things stood at home. Then he might call in a favor and see what he could find out about the local sheriff's office. And Margaret. Dammit, he needed her to be home, not gallivanting off to New York. He might even be able to park Kit with her for a few days, just until she got her life back on track.

Kit's life, not Margaret's. Margaret's life had been on track ever since she'd decorated his tree house with curtains made from dust rags, pictures torn out of *Good Housekeeping,* and replaced his Keep Out sign with a worn-out welcome mat.

Carson was dozing when Kit tiptoed into the room. Standing over him, a towel wrapped around her wet hair, she studied the man who had become such an important part of her life in less than a week. Less than half a week.

Good Lord, had it been only two-and-a-half-going-on-three days?

She dealt in fiction, not fantasy, but if she ever wanted to try her hand at fairy tales, she knew who her Prince Charming would be. And with a bit of role reversal, just how she would awaken him.

His eyes opened suddenly. Kit stepped back, tripped over the shoe she'd stepped out of before going into the bathroom, and flailed her arms. "Dad-blast it—darned shoe! I'm sorry, I didn't mean to wake you."

Sitting up, he flexed his shoulders, and she realized that as rocky as she still felt, he looked as if he felt even worse. He must think she was crazy, the way she'd been hovering over him, staring down while he slept as if she were trying to put a curse on him or something.

What was the feminine version of voyeur? Voyeuress?

"There's a row of machines down at the other end," he said, his voice verging on raw. "While I'm still dressed, I could check it out if you're interested."

She shook her head. Her stomach was fidgeting after only a few bites of that sub. Not queasy, just tense. "I'm fine, but thanks. There's plenty of hot water left, but not much soap. I used almost a whole bar on my hair. There wasn't any shampoo, just two measly bars of soap, but I had to get rid of the smoke smell."

"No problem. We'll go shopping first thing in the morning."

"I might not wake up real early. Can we get a wake-up call?"

"Why bother? First one up wakes the other, and we'll go from there."

He stood, stretched and massaged his temples. Kit had stepped back, but the room was small. Smoke, clean male sweat and red hot peppers. Bottle it, and you'd have the world's most effective aphrodisiac.

Quickly, before she could blurt out anything embarrassing, she turned and folded down the covers. Kicking her shoes aside, she climbed into bed and pulled the covers up around her ears. If she pretended to be asleep when he came back, she might be able to stay out of trouble.

His shirt was off before he closed the bathroom door behind him, revealing a tanned, wedge-shaped back with a few intriguing scars, which she did her best to ignore. Yawning, she closed her eyes and tried to focus on re-creating the story of *Gretchen's Ghost* from the first line.

It was a lost cause. The picture that emerged on her mental screen resembled an X-rated video—one that left her feeling flushed and restless.

Eleven

Sometime during the night another line of thunderstorms came through. Hard rain pelted the window. Lightning flashed, and a loud blast of thunder brought Kit instantly wide-awake. Carson was beside her in an instant. "Shh, hush, honey, it's only thunder."

Carson had been awake for the past hour, sorting through the mess they'd left back at Gilbert's Point. Trying to keep his mind off the woman in the next bed—a woman who was becoming far too important to him on the basis of a two-and-a-half day acquaintance.

Trying to keep from doing what he was doing now, which was climbing into her bed. Maybe not in it, but close enough.

"I know that," she shot back in a breathless whisper, but her pulse was going a mile a minute. "I'm not afraid of storms, I was dreaming—something about an explosion...I think."

Holding her against him, he rocked back and forth. All he could think of to say was, "There, there," and it wasn't enough. With everything that had happened to her—happened around her, at least—it was no wonder she had nightmares.

He'd had the occasional nightmare, himself. But then, he was a cop. He'd seen far worse things than drug-related shootings. He'd been out of the picture for several weeks during which time family matters had become increasingly important. He might have lost his edge.

Then again, he might simply have lost his mind.

Minutes passed, minutes during which Carson became increasingly aware of the heat of her body, the delicacy of her bones—aware of other things he tried hard to ignore. Like the heat rising from her skin, the scent of motel soap and warm, sleepy woman, and that subtle fruity-spicy fragrance that was hers alone. He could've sworn there was nothing that smelled like that among the amenities provided by the establishment.

She was wearing his T-shirt. He didn't know what she was wearing underneath—didn't want to know.

God, talk about an imagination! Maybe he should try his hand at writing fiction. The kind of fiction that was passed around and snickered over by adolescent males.

Down, boy! Wrong time, wrong woman, wrong circumstances.

Her cold hands were moving up and down his sides. They did little to cool the rising heat of his body. Neither did the fact that he was sitting on the side of her bed, twisted into an awkward position that was going to put a crick in his back if he didn't shift pretty soon—preferably to a horizontal position. Kit had somehow managed to come up on her knees, the covers trailing around her hips, her head, shoulders and hands touching him while her tidy little rear end was aimed in the opposite direction.

"Aren't you, uh, uncomfortable?" he ventured.

"Just cold. I can't seem to stop shivering." He was still working on an excuse to hand over some money and make a run for the border when she said, "Please? Bad things always make me cold. When the police came to tell me about Mama and Father, I thought I'd never be warm again."

Yeah, talk about her family, he thought desperately. Talk about the weather—about anything to get his mind off his rampaging hormones. She called her folks Mama and Father? That said something about their relationship.

Her hair tickled his face. In brushing it away, he encountered an ear, minus the usual hardware. Tonight it had been a couple of miniature chandeliers, which she'd removed before heading for the shower.

Talk, man, talk! As long as you're talking you can't get into too much trouble. "Why did the police come to tell you? Why not inform your grandparents and let them break the news?"

"They were on a cruise. They flew back from Cozumel and—and…"

Yeah, he could imagine. They'd probably been about as comforting as an empty ice tray. He ran his hands over her hair—soft, warm, alive—and made soothing noises, realizing as he did so that he had somehow shifted position until he was more or less horizontal.

And so was she.

Good thing he was still outside the covers.

But then, so was she. And she was no longer shivering.

Ah, jeez, he needed some kind of a fire wall here. A few thin layers of cotton weren't going to do it. His T-shirt, his boxers, plus whatever she was wearing underneath. Which wasn't much. She wasn't wearing a bra, that much was obvious. When he went to ease her away so that he could think clearly, the back of his hand brushed across her small, soft breast. The nipple stood up like a ripe cherry, begging to be plucked.

Okay, this is not personal, parts of his brain that were still functioning insisted. The woman woke up in a nightmare and he just happened to be the closest thing at hand, right?

Wrong. Trouble had been brewing between them from the first moment he'd seen her clearly, leaning over him to see if she'd killed him or merely broken a few more bones.

"Honey, don't you think—" he began when she cut him off.

"I don't want to think. Not now...please."

That made two of them. Holding her against him, he struggled for objectivity, trying to ignore the perfect alignment of their bodies. "Okay, I can understand that." Was that his voice? It sounded as if his collar was about two sizes too small. "Just try to think about..."

About what? Home?

She didn't have one.

Her writing career?

According to what she'd told him she'd just had three months work wiped out. He didn't know if that ended her career, or what. He knew about as much about the writing profession as he did about ballet. Less, in fact. His folks had taken him to a performance of *Swan Lake* when he was twelve years old. He'd liked the girls, been interested in the athletics and had been terrified that one of his buddies would see him there.

They could talk about family. That had always been his bolthole when he was working a particularly ugly case.

As soon as it was over he'd buy a six-pack, head for his folks' house, using the side gate to reach his mother's garden, where he could sit and get quietly drunk. Listening to the birds, bugs and tree frogs always reminded him that there were still pockets of sanity left in the world.

Sometimes he needed reminding.

So he held her. If she needed an anchor, he could be here for her, at least until she was able to stand alone. Never mind his testosterone overload. It wasn't this woman in particular. Couldn't be. He hadn't known her long enough. No way would he take advantage of any woman just because they happened to be in bed together, sharing a single set of underwear. No way.

She had no way of knowing that he'd been going through a long, dry spell. Hadn't had sex since he'd more or less made up his mind to marry Margaret, and as theirs wasn't that kind of a relationship, he was long overdue some relief. His fault, maybe, for letting her get away with one postponement after another, but then, he hadn't exactly been in shape for a honeymoon.

Meanwhile, Kate, his mother, went right on cutting and pasting, humming snatches of wedding music. Of course, she also kept on washing her china plates, drying them and stacking them on a table out in the front hall. None of them could figure out what that was all about.

"If you're cold, we could get under the covers," Kit suggested.

He stiffened. All over. "Honey, I don't think that's such a good idea. I mean, it's late and we have a big day coming up, and besides..."

"Oh. I forgot about your sort-of Margaret." Her attempt to laugh was so pathetic it hurt. She said, "I still smell like smoke. Sorry. Forget it. Rotten idea."

"Kit—"

"Go to bed. I'm fine now, I just had a bad dream."

Yeah, like he could just forget the whole thing and fall asleep anytime within the next decade. He was determined to make the effort, though.

And he did. Made the effort to sit up, at least.

"I just wish you weren't sort-of engaged," she said so softly he wasn't sure he'd heard her at first.

And he thought, so do I, sweetheart. Oh, God, so do I!

The truth was, Carson was feeling less and less as if this arrangement with Margaret was going to be anything other than a disaster. Just because they'd known each other all their lives—just because neither of them had anyone else on the string, he'd thought they could make it work for his mother's sake. They both loved Kate, even if they didn't love each other. As friends, maybe, but he was beginning to realize that friendly love wasn't enough. Not when he could feel this way about another woman.

"I'm not actually engaged," he said, and then felt like a rotten, opportunistic skunk. "I mean we sort of had this understanding—for my mother's sake." Weasel mouth! "Look, I won't lie to you, Kit, right now I'd like nothing more than to spend the rest of the night—hell, make that the rest of the week—making love to you."

Making love? A voice mocked. You mean having sex, don't you?

Love didn't enter into the equation. No way. Too soon. Didn't make sense, he told himself as the heat of their joined bodies eddied up around them, sweet, musky and enticing.

"Me, too," she said so softly he had to lean down to hear her.

And that was all it took. Because her mouth was there, and so was his, and once they touched, the rest was inevitable. Later he might tell himself that they'd both been

needy, if for different reasons, but at that moment, reason
was the last thing on his mind. He was driven by sheer,
blind lust for a woman he'd been attracted to almost from
the first. Which was so absurd he would have laughed if
he hadn't been feeling so damned desperate.

She tasted the way she smelled, like ripe fruit with a
hint of spice. Not smoky at all. Inside, she was warm and
needy, and so was he. In twisting around, the shirt she
was wearing had ridden up so that her silken body rubbed
against his, and she didn't feel cold at all. Just the opposite.

She twisted against him, and he groaned without removing his mouth from hers. More than lust—maybe not
love, but far more than lust. The thought whipped through
his mind and slipped away before he could deny it.

"Kit...?"

Kit knew what he was asking. *Are you sure?*

"I'm sure," she said firmly in answer to the unasked
question. Or as firmly as she could when she was quaking
inside like a bowl of jelly. Not from nerves—well, maybe
from nerves, but from something else, too. She had read
about the effect of acute desire, but never felt it before,
not to this degree. Never even imagined it. Not that she
hadn't done sex, because she had. Three times, in fact.
She'd found it messy, uncomfortable and just a little bit
boring. Eating popcorn and watching a good movie was
far more exciting.

But the moment she'd touched this man's hard, dry
palm when she'd been trying to pull him to his feet before
he slid into the ditch, she'd felt as if every cell in her
body had suddenly come alive. Felt a stab of awareness
that tickled her in places where she'd never been tickled
before. Actually, tickle didn't exactly describe the sensa-

tion, but it was close enough. Too close, considering how
terrified she'd been at the time.

"If you want to back out, you can," she felt obliged
to say, because she had more or less seduced the man.
Done her best, at least. "My feelings won't be hurt. My
goodness, I am an adult, after all."

"Sure you are," he mocked softly.

Kit could have argued, but right now that was the last
thing she wanted to do. She sighed as his warm hand
closed over her breast. He'd rolled over onto his side and
was looking at her, his gaze lingering on the lower part
of her body, clad only in the brief cotton underpants she'd
worn under her dress. The heat in his eyes seared a path-
way, causing her to catch a shuddering breath.

It would help if he weren't so beautiful. She couldn't
remember ever thinking of a man's body as being beautiful. Actually, she hadn't thought much about men's
bodies at all, other than the normal curiosity of any young
woman. Since the age of eighteen she'd been far too busy
scrambling to support herself by waiting tables and writing and illustrating the stories that had begun taking shape
in her mind back in her closet days.

Carson Beckett was beautiful. Scars and all. Beautiful
from the soles of his high-arched feet with the dusting of
dark hair on top, to his beard-shadowed face with the
twisty mouth, those incredibly blue eyes and the twin ver-
tical lines that creased his lean cheeks.

Leaning away, he gave her a worried look. "Kit, you're
not—that is, you're not a, uh—?"

"A virgin? Oh, for goodness' sake, of course not. I'm
twenty-five years old, Carson."

"Right. I just needed to be sure."

The fact that he'd even thought it possible was probably
insulting, but with his breath warm on her hair, his hands

making magic circles on her quivering middle, she chose not to be insulted.

Besides, he'd asked. Some men wouldn't have been so sensitive. The man who'd taken her virginity hadn't.

And then the past was swept away, along with any lingering doubts she might have briefly harbored. She gasped, covering his hand with her own as his fingers hooked under the elastic of her high-cut panties. He kissed her again, sipping like a butterfly, dipping in again and again for the nectar. Frantic with need, she stroked him wherever she could reach, savoring the feel of his lean, taut waist, his narrow hips, and wishing she dared touch him *there*.

A small sound—part groan, part whimper, escaped her. As if it were the catalyst he needed, Carson covered her mound with his palm, cupping his fingers between her thighs. The T-shirt was twisted around her, baring her breasts, but wadded uncomfortably under her shoulders. How the devil was she supposed to get rid of her clothes? There was no graceful way to do it now, and she hadn't had the forethought to remove them before. If there was some sort of protocol to this business of sex, she wished she'd taken time to read the rule book.

Evidently Carson had read it. Sliding one hand under the elastic and the other against her hips, he lifted her and slid her panties down her bare legs. Tossing them away, he kissed the arch of her bare foot and she nearly screamed.

Next he eased the shirt over her head and discarded it. Clasping her face between his hands, he searched her eyes in the indirect light as if to read any lingering doubts there. It was all she could do not to beg him to get on with it. Not to blurt out words she knew instinctively he didn't want to hear. If she hadn't been certain before this—and she hadn't, because there'd been too much else crowded into the past two days—she knew now that she could never get enough of this man. The taste of him, the feel of him—the way he tried to protect her even when she suspected that all he wanted was to be rid of her and her problems, that had nothing to do with him.

If that wasn't love, it was too close for comfort.

And if this was all she could ever have of him, then she would take it and live on the memory.

"Kit? Where are you, sweetheart? Don't disappear on me now."

"I'm right here," she breathed.

"If you don't want this, then say so. I'll live. Might be a while before I can walk upright, but I'll survive."

If she didn't want it? She was little more than a molten puddle of liquid desire, couldn't he tell? "Do you have a thingee?" she asked, trying to sound suave and experienced.

He leaned up onto one elbow and stared at her. "A what?"

"You know—a condom." Oh, lord, woman, don't blush now!

He collapsed onto the pillow, and for a minute she thought he was laughing. But then he slipped out of bed, retrieved his wallet from the khakis he'd tossed across the chair, and within seconds he was back again.

But not before she'd had time to enjoy the view. Men were built so different from women. Their hips cupped in on the sides. Hers, even as skinny as she was, went out. Like a snake that had just swallowed an egg. Make that one egg and two raisins, because she had breasts. They might be small, but they were all her own.

Lifting the cover, he eased back underneath. "Honey, I don't want to rush you, but…"

She laughed, and if there was a slight edge of hysteria in the sound, then it was hardly any wonder. If she'd written the story of everything that had happened these past forty-eight hours and tried to sell it to a publisher, they'd have laughed her off the planet.

"Go ahead, rush me," she said, opening her arms.

He came down to her then, holding his weight up on both arms while he searched her face once more, as if needing to reassure himself that she hadn't changed her mind. Not in a millions years, she wanted to tell him, but had sense enough for once to keep quiet.

He said, "I'm so hungry for you I'm afraid I might hurt you. It's, uh—been awhile for me."

"Me, too. I won't break." As if to prove it, she pulled him down on top of her. He began to kiss her again, parting her lips, thrusting—taking all she had to give and hungrily demanding more. Then he nibbled a trail down the side of her throat, paving the way with his hands until he reached her breasts.

At the hot rasp of his tongue on her nipple, an explosion of pleasure so sharp it was almost pain streaked through her. Searching with her fingertips, she combed through the crisp hair on his chest until she encountered the twin nubs of hardened flesh.

A shudder racked his body. "Sweetheart, I'm on a short fuse, and it's burning fast."

It was all she could do not to cry out her own fierce need as, easing her thighs apart, he positioned himself between them, the hair-roughened texture of his skin strangely exciting against her sensitive inner thighs. Unable to stop herself, she reached down between their bodies and touched him there. Lightning stabbed her again as her hand closed around hot steel, sheathed in velvet.

She snatched her hand away, and then she felt him

brush against her entrance. She was embarrassingly wet. Had he noticed? Why was he hesitating? She was about to explode and he hadn't even entered her yet. Was it possible for a woman to climax before a man was even inside her? Never in her wildest dreams. Certainly not in her limited experience.

And then he pushed inside her and she bit back a scream. Colors—she saw it in colors, like a pulsating rainbow magnified a thousand times. Frantically, she sought words to describe it, because she was a writer, after all, and words were her tools.

Right. It felt so *right*.

Then he began to move, and it felt even more right. She was acutely aware of every inch of her flesh—and of his.

His eyes were closed, his face harsh, almost masklike. His shoulders were trembling, and she sensed he was fighting against the inevitable. She didn't want to fight, she wanted to let it happen. Let it wash over her, like an enormous neon-colored surf.

Teeth bared in a grimace, he thrust harder, quicker. She thought he spoke her name, but then the bonds of pleasure began tightening around her, lifting her up, tearing her apart. A chorus of angels could have shouted her name and she wouldn't have heeded. She tried to grasp his shoulders, but her hands slid off his sweat-slick flesh. She tried to meet his thrusts, but her timing was off, and then it was too late because she was drowning, drowning...

Somewhere inside her head, a voice whispered caution, but she was beyond heeding. Eons beyond. Wrapped in the arms of the man she loved—the man who had to feel more than mere lust for her, because Fate wouldn't be so cruel, Kit slept. And dreamed.

Twelve

It was barely light outside when Carson awoke. One moment he was deeply asleep, the next instant he was wide-awake, partly due to training, partly due to his own nature. He had an agenda that couldn't wait any longer.

Quietly, he checked his cell phone to be sure the battery had recharged overnight. It was too early to call home, but by the time he showered and dressed, and slipped outside to see what the machines had in the way of breakfast, enough time would have passed. He had other calls to make first.

He managed to get as far as the door some ten minutes later before Kit began to stir. Turning, he gazed down at the woman who had come to mean too much to him at a time when he didn't have room for another woman in his life. He hated to leave her. Even with the note, she might misunderstand. But a man had to do what a man had to do. What sage had said that? Someone good at rationalizing, obviously.

A few minutes later he sat in the front seat of the Yukon, sipping an orange-flavored drink that bore little resemblance to any known citrus fruit while he punched in a number that was not on automatic dial.

"Moose? Beckett here. Look, I'm sorry to—" He listened for a moment, then broke into the litany. "Yeah, I caught it, too, thanks to Mac. Not too bad, though. Twenty-four hours and I'm back in fighting form." Sure he was. "Listen, I need you to check out a guy for me. I'm in North Carolina, in—" He glanced at the highway map and filled in the vital information. "Sheriff and two deputies. I need a line on one of the deputies, a guy by the name of Junius Mooney. Right. He's a new-hire deputy, been here about six months from what I understand. I don't know where he came from, and I'm not particularly eager to start asking around, if you know what I mean."

After answering a few more questions, Carson clicked off and moved to his next call. Punching in the automatic dial number, he glanced toward the closed door of unit 8. No sign of activity yet. She needed her sleep. He needed her to sleep.

Deliberately fire-walling all thought of the past several hours, he waited for someone to catch the phone. His mother would still be asleep, but the nurse would be up.

So, evidently, was his father. "Hi, Pop? Listen, how's Mom?" A few minutes later he said, "No, I'm not back home yet—still in North Carolina. What I want to know is—no, I haven't heard from Margaret, but—" He broke off and listened for perhaps a full minute.

Ah, jeez. "Did she say where she could be reached?"

Well, that was that, he thought a few minutes later, after

promising to check back and let his folks know what his plans were.

At this point, he hadn't a clue. All he knew was that he couldn't leave Kit here alone. Couldn't leave her at all until this mess was cleared up. He had no obligation and even less legal authority, but as long as she was vulnerable, he couldn't walk away.

Which presented a whole new set of problems.

Inside the motel room, Kit opened her eyes and stared at the ceiling, trying to wrap her mind around events of the immediate past. The one thing that impressed her above all else was a certain feeling of…hollowness. Emptiness, as if something she'd briefly possessed had been snatched away.

She flexed her ankles, still stiff from wobbling around on those designer shoes, the designer being the Marquis de Sade. Sliding her legs over the edge of the bed, she sat up, glancing toward the open bathroom door.

"Carson?" He could be shaving, she told herself, knowing that if he were anywhere nearby, she would have sensed it. Forcing herself to stay calm, to think logically, she murmured aloud, "Take a deep breath. Forget what happened, it's over, okay? Time to move on."

She waited for the words to sink in.

It didn't help. Dammit—damn it all to hell and back, she didn't want to move on! At least, if she moved anywhere, she didn't want to do it alone.

I never promised you a rose ga-arden. Words to the corny old song played over in her mind, and she bit her lip to keep from laughing. Or maybe from crying.

Instead she cursed some more, awkwardly and inexpertly, and then she flung back the covers and stood. And there on the bedside table next to the telephone, was a can of orange-flavored drink, a packaged muffin and a sack of corn chips.

And a note. Blinking the sleep from her eyes, she scanned the few lines. His handwriting was half-printing, half-script. It looked just like the man himself—hard-edged, but with a grace and softness that was rare among men—at least the men of her acquaintance.

She read, "It's 6:47 a.m., Sleeping Beauty. I'll be back in a couple of hours with stuff we need. Change of clothes and some real food. List everything you remember that happened, everything you lost in the fire and anything else that needs listing." In other words, she translated, keep your mind occupied so you won't panic.

Well, that was just too damned tough. If she wanted to panic, she would damn well panic. And curse while she was doing it. She might be a flake—she'd been called it more than a few times—but no one had ever called her a wimp.

She read the last hastily scribbled line. "You might want to call your folks and let them know where you are." He signed it C. B. No Love, no Sincerely—no nothing. Just his damn-blasted initials.

She didn't start crying until she went into the bathroom and saw her panties and bra hanging over the shower rod, where he had rinsed them out and hung them to dry. She took them down—they were still damp—and rolled them in the last clean hand towel.

She might have sobbed a time or two standing under the stream of hot water, but at least she didn't gulp water and drown. By the time she stepped out and wrapped herself in a skimpy bath towel, she felt marginally better. Or if not better, at least more in command.

Lists? He wanted her to make lists?

Fine. She could start with the fact that she was staying

in a motel she couldn't pay for, with no place to go if she left, and no way of getting there even if she had a place to go. There was a single ten-dollar bill tucked into her evening purse, a comb and some loose change; a driver's license, her social security card and slim ballpoint pen. So yes, she could make a list, but of what? Her prospects? Her worldly possessions?

Ha! Short list.

And that wasn't even the worst of it. Sometime in the past few days she had taken complete leave of her senses and fallen madly in love with a man who was engaged to another woman, a man who had a sick mother who needed him—a man who claimed in his note that he'd be back, but then, why should he? He was under no obligation just because they had—

Well. He might have mentioned taking her home with him, but that had been a social lie. She knew all about those. She'd been hearing them all her life—lies designed to protect the flawless Dixon facade of old money and old family her grandfather so loved to project.

The fact that neither the money nor the family had been his didn't faze him. His father had been a greengrocer in Cincinnati, and he'd earned scholarships to get through law school.

Kit toyed with the pen, staring at the blank page on the motel's notepad. If she had to call her grandfather, she would do it. It was marginally preferable to hitchhiking. She could call Jeff, but he really couldn't afford to leave work, not when she'd left him shorthanded, and besides, Gilbert's Point was the last place she wanted to go now.

Dressed in the fuchsia satin, which was all she had to put on, with her damp, freshly combed hair woven into a lumpy braid, she was sitting on the fake leather armchair, her feet propped on the bed, with half a glass of orange-colored liquid beside her when the door rattled and then opened. She'd started her list by drawing a big, fat number one and doodling all around it.

Doodling. The creative mind at work.

"You should've fastened the chain as soon as you got up," Carson said.

"The door was locked." Where have you been? I thought you weren't coming back!

"You got any idea how easy it is to get into one of these rooms?" He tossed several large bags onto the bed and carefully placed another one on the table beside her. "Chain's not much good. One hard shove and the screws pop out. Here, I brought us some breakfast."

She had eaten half the muffin and all of the corn chips he'd left her and she was still starved. "It's my metabolism," she said defiantly, irrationally angry because she thought he'd left her here and gone home. "Creative people burn calories just thinking."

"Right," he said with a quizzical lift of one crow-black eyebrow.

Kit opened the bag and took out a lidded cup of coffee, a greasy, white-flour biscuit filled with all sorts of wicked things, and a big, sugar-topped raisin bun. "Oh, I'm in heaven," she said with a sigh, eagerly unwrapping the bun.

Not until the sweet was half-demolished did she notice that Carson wasn't wearing the clothes he'd left in. Instead he had on a new pair of jeans that were darker than the softly faded, close-fitting ones he'd worn that first day. The black knit shirt was similar, and he was wearing the same brown leather boots, minus most of the mud and soot from the night before.

"Do you ride?" she asked, licking the sugar off her thumb.

"Do I what?"

"You know—horses." She took another bite and nodded to his feet.

"Oh. Horses. Yeah, I used to ride. Haven't in a long time, though. The boots are purely an affectation."

"Ha. You're the least affected man I know. You don't even wear cologne."

"Hey, I'm a detective, right? Hard to sneak up on the bad guys when they can smell you coming a mile away."

She grinned and started unwrapping her ham-egg-and-cheese biscuit. And here she'd thought she would never laugh again. Given enough sugar in her system, she could conquer the world.

Or at least Currituck County. "Randolph—you remember Randolph from the party? He wears some scent that he modestly lets everyone on the planet know he had custom blended just for him." She concentrated on her biscuit. Concentrated on anything and everything that would keep her from dwelling on the immediate future.

He didn't say a word. He was obviously going to let her wallow in embarrassment just because she'd practically dragged him into her bed.

She took a big bite of her breakfast sandwich and chewed savagely, glaring down at the fuchsia satin, cabbage-sized rose on her left knee.

"What's the matter, is it cold? I don't think they have microwaves here, but I could ask in the office."

"It's not the sandwich," she said with a dismissive shrug.

"Yeah, well...when you're finished eating, you might want to try on the stuff I bought. We can exchange anything that doesn't fit, but I thought you might want something else to wear while you shop for the rest of what you need for the next few days. I'm no good at picking out women's whatchamacallits.''

"Oh, am I going shopping?" Her smile was about as genuine as a two-dollar diamond ring. Stop it. Just stop it right now. He's trying to be decent, and you're acting like a spoiled brat!

Carson hiked up his stiff new jeans and sat on the edge of the bed. "First you're going to finish eating," he said. "Then you're going to change clothes and then we're going to talk. After that we'll go shopping."

Before he could issue further orders, his cell phone buzzed softly. Kit pried the lid off her coffee, still steaming but weak as water, while Carson turned away.

"Yeah, Moose? You got something for me?"

Moose? She tried not to listen, she really did. Besides, he was mostly listening. Why bother to eavesdrop on someone who spoke only in monosyllables? Halfway through the one-sided conversation he leaned over and started making notes on the list she had started and forgotten.

She tried to remember what was on it. The fat number one followed by a lot of doodling. Nothing incriminating, thank goodness—she was pretty certain of that. No hearts and flowers, with the initials C.B. entwined with K.D.

"Thanks, man," he said, and realizing that she was leaning over to see what he'd jotted down, she sat up straight. "I owe you," he said into a phone no larger than a pack of cigarettes. "What? Probably next week, so get your butt out of my chair, y'hear?"

He punched off, laid the phone aside, thumbed up a sandwich crumb from the napkin on the table and licked it off. "I bought this ergonomic chair when I had some back trouble. Now every guy in the department wants one just like it."

Kit's fingers crept back toward the notepad. She'd seen just enough to remember what she'd doodled there. A pair of high-heeled sandals bracketed by a pair of cowboy boots.

I'll die. I'll just crawl off somewhere and die quietly, and by the time he gets back to Charleston he'll have forgotten my name.

"Okay, you ready to talk now?"

She swallowed the lump in her throat and set aside the uneaten half of her biscuit. "Do we have to?"

"I thought you wanted answers."

"That depends on the questions."

"For starters, how about who shot Tank Hubble, and why? How about who torched your house, and why? But I guess you pretty well figured out that one for yourself."

"To scare me off, you mean."

Carson let it go at that. She didn't really need to be reminded that she and poor old Hubble fell into the same category, not after what had happened to Tank. He didn't know how serious the attempts on her life had been, or how far they would have gone, but even the dumbest perps occasionally pulled off a hit and got away with it. It happened more than the general public suspected.

As it turned out in this particular case, Internal Affairs had started closing in on their rogue deputy shortly before Kit had spotted his truck and spooked. But not before he'd had time to get rid of one witness and made a couple of unsuccessful attempts to silence the second witness.

"Turns out you were right on target," he said. "Mooney has been under surveillance ever since discrepancies started showing up, mostly concerning missing evidence."

"Missing evidence of what?"

"Dope and guns, taken in other busts. Supposedly kept under lock and key."

He could practically see her processing the information. Oh, yeah—the lady was a lot smarter than she let on. He was onto her now.

She took a big gulp of coffee and wrinkled her nose. Not a sign of makeup, Carson marveled, watching her, and she was flat-out gorgeous. Naked freckles, shadowed eyes, messy hair and all.

"Kit, Kit," he said softly. Rising, he stood over her, removed the cup from her hand and lifted her to her feet. "What am I going to do with you?" he whispered.

She was barely breathing—but then, he was having trouble in that regard, too. His heart was pounding a mile a minute, but he clean forgot to breathe. She lifted her face as naturally as a sunflower sought out the sun, and he met her halfway. Her lips parted under his, the liquid dance of desire, lightly seasoned with coffee, escalating as his hands moved over her satin-clad body.

Digging her fingers under his belt, Kit tried to pull his shirttail free, as if desperately needing to touch bare skin. Needing...everything.

"You've got clothes to try on, woman," he said gruffly, but neither of them seriously thought there'd be any trying-on in the near future.

At least, not of clothes.

By the time they ended up in bed, along with a shoebox and several bags, Kit had somehow managed to shed her dress. Getting Carson out of his stiff new jeans took more time. Took four hands and a lot of awkward, breathless maneuvers. The jeans weren't all that was stiff.

"You're downright habit-forming," he murmured once they were both suitably naked. His mouth moved down her throat toward her breasts. "Either that or—" he laved one nipple with his tongue, relishing her reaction ''—or my immune system is seriously compromised.''

''You're accusing me of compromising you?'' she teased.

''Oh, yea-ahhh…'' This time they took time to savor each small step along the way. Bolder now, Kit insisted on exploring, and Carson lay back and allowed her to have her way with him. Actually encouraged it in so many words, his own passion enhanced, if that were possible, by her obvious delight.

''May I kiss you here?'' she asked, toying with one of his nipples. His heart lodged somewhere in his throat while his lungs threatened to go on strike.

''What about here?'' she asked moments later as she probed his navel, then traced the scattering of dark hair surrounding it.

Swallowing hard, he managed to nod. ''Be my guest.''

Some time later, she moved south, having evidently gained courage from his reaction to her earlier ministrations.

This time, the instant her hand closed around him, he covered it with his own. ''Wait—just—give me a minute,'' he gasped.

And so she gave him a minute—maybe two before she reclaimed control. And then Carson returned the favor. It was hours before either of them thought about going shopping again.

Thirteen

After explaining to Kit about the internal investigation, Carson checked in with the local sheriff again, leaving a number where he and Kit could be reached in the event it became necessary. She didn't question him. She did give him a look he found impossible to interpret.

After that they went shopping, as he'd just picked up the bare essentials on his earlier foray. Shopping was not something he'd ever enjoyed, unless it was shopping for fishing tackle. Shopping with a woman was in a totally different category.

It turned out to involve lots of laughter and a few minor skirmishes, but no real problems. He insisted on buying her a pair of plain navy jeans and a white camp shirt.

"Dull, dull, dull! May I at least pick out my own accessories?"

Feeling magnanimous—feeling, in fact, as if he'd just tossed back one too many glasses of vintage champagne, he said, "Be my guest. I'll meet you here in what—ten minutes?" Here being the book section of the big discount store, where Kit had looked over the children's section and sighed, but hadn't said anything.

Thirty-five minutes later she was back, proudly showing off a pair of red sandals, some purple knee socks and wearing a pair of bead-and-feather earrings that dusted her shoulders. "I bought these on my own," she announced, touching them proudly, "so don't say a word. I needed something to cheer me up."

He only shook his head and grinned. This was Kit. His Kit, whether or not she knew it. He'd caught onto her by now. The more uncertain she felt on the inside, the more outrageous she acted on the outside. Methinks thou dost protest too much...hadn't somebody or other once said something like that?

Yeah, she had her defense mechanism, but then, so did he.

Once outside the store, they surveyed the lunch possibilities and decided on subs again. After the first few protests, Kit didn't mention paying him back. He knew she was only biding her time—knew, too, that at the moment, she had few options, at least until they could reestablish her credentials and cash her check.

They left the sub shop and set out across the rapidly filling parking lot toward his car. She said, "Okay, what next? Where do we go from here?"

He unlocked the doors and thought of how best to put it. What had been a disaster for her had turned out to be a windfall for him, but he didn't think she was ready to hear that, and so he asked her for a favor. "Kit, I need you to think seriously about coming home with me."

When she started to protest, he held up a hand. They were still standing outside the car under a cloudless sky.

He should have bought her some sunglasses. "Now wait," he said. "Just hear me out before you say anything."

She crossed her arms and waited. Her left foot was starting to tap. "I'm listening." Was this the same woman who had come apart in his arms again and again, only a few hours ago?

"Yeah, but with a closed mind, right? Kit—look, it's early yet. I mean, in days. For us, I mean." Smooth, Beckett. Real smooth. "But you have to admit, things have been kind of crazy ever since we met."

She nodded. "That much I'll grant you."

Carson rubbed the back of his neck. As a busted-up cop with too many years of rough mileage on him, he was in no position to blurt out his feelings. They were too new. Truth was, they scared the hell out of him, and he'd never been called a coward. Been called a few other things, but never a coward. "Okay, here goes," he said, eyes narrowed, fists on his hips. "I want you to come home with me as my fiancée. Wait—wait." He held up a hand. "Don't say anything yet. We can get married as soon as you round up a dress—something fancy with a veil—maybe kind of old-fashioned. Margaret can show you where to shop and all. And then—"

"Margaret? *Your* Margaret?"

"She's not my Margaret—at least, not the way you mean it. Look, we were never in love. Never could have been, not in a million years, we know each other too well. But we were willing to go through with a wedding for my mom's sake. Because we both love her and it's the last thing we can do for her to bring her any joy. But then Margaret got this chance to join a New York decorating—"

"Wait! Just hold on—you're trying to tell me Margaret

dumped you and now you want me to marry you? Just like that?''

Raking a hand through his hair, Carson turned away and stared at a heavily detailed monster truck on display near the center of the parking lot. Man, talk about screwing up! He'd never got around to formally proposing to Margaret, but when he'd first broached the subject of a marriage for his mother's sake, he'd done it at Margaret's favorite French restaurant. He'd wanted every advantage he could scratch up. Not that it had done much good. In the first place, he didn't like food he could neither recognize nor pronounce. In the second place, he'd been without sleep for almost thirty-six hours.

To make up for that and a few more shortcomings, he'd bought her two dozen roses.

She'd started sneezing.

''Okay, so maybe this isn't the most romantic place for a proposal. I just wanted to let you know you had another option. Besides calling on the judge, I mean.''

She snorted. No other word for it. He didn't know if it was his proposal, which might have been somewhat lacking in finesse, or the mention of her grandfather. ''You're talking about a marriage of convenience,'' she stated.

''I am?''

''Well, what else would it be?''

''Legal, for one thing. As for the rest, I guess you could say it's negotiable.'' He had a feeling he was headed down a dead-end road, but wasn't quite sure when he'd taken the wrong turn.

''Get in the car,'' he said. ''I can't stand too long in one position without my knee acting up.''

Man, you are a real prize. Why not play on her sympathy? It worked before—she took you in after nearly running you off the road.

To hell with that. "Okay, let's cut to the chase. I need you, and you need—"

"No, I don't." Arms still crossed, foot still tapping. Eyes flashing danger signs that could be picked up by any spy satellite.

Oh, what the hell, man—if you're going to blow it, might as well blow the works. "Yeah, honey, you do. But not as much as I need you, and if you want to know the truth, it's not just because my mother happens to be hung up on weddings." She swallowed hard. That was an encouraging sign, wasn't it? "So I thought maybe if we start out slow—play things by ear for a while—I mean, go through with the ceremony and all, but my house has two bedrooms. We can set you up in one with a bed and a desk. I'll get you a computer and whatever art supplies you need and you can—"

"Carson?"

"—back up your works, and maybe even write faster. I don't know how it works with the kind of writing you do, but cleaning up mistakes is bound to be faster, so—"

"Carson?"

"—so anyhow, I'll be at work mostly, and you can have the place all to yourself. It'd be nice if you dropped by to visit my mom every few days, but that's up to you."

"Carson!"

Carson heard laughter and glanced around at a handful of shoppers loading parcels into a green pickup two slots over. He looked back at Kit and felt his face grow hot. "Yeah? Sorry—I guess we'd better continue this discussion somewhere else."

"How about our room?"

Our room. *Our* room? He hadn't checked out yet,

knowing that if things didn't work out, he'd have to fall back on a hastily formed contingency plan.

Without another word they climbed into the Yukon and buckled up. Carson started the engine, drove approximately fifteen feet and stopped. He pulled on the emergency brake. "Listen, I may as well level with you. It's not fair, me asking you to go into this thing not knowing the score."

She looked at him as if he were an interesting specimen of insect and she couldn't decide whether to step on him or let him live. Strong woman. She might look like a flake, he thought, not for the first time, but there was a core of tempered steel underneath that gaudy, irresistible facade.

"I'm listening," she said.

Oh boy. Crunch time. "I, uh—I've never done this before, so I might screw up."

"Never done what? Stop traffic in the middle of a parking lot on a busy Saturday afternoon?"

Behind him, a car horn blared out. "Wait a sec," he growled and pulled over to one side, beside the gardening display.

He shut off the engine, unsnapped his seat belt, turned to her and said, "Okay, here's the score. I think I might be in love with you. If that scares you, I promise never to mention it again, but—"

"Carson."

"—but I just thought you ought to know going in what you're up against. I mean, I really like you, too. Like and respect—"

"Carson?"

"So we could start out as friends, maybe go on like that for a few days—that is, a few weeks. Or even longer—it's your call." Not that he wouldn't be doing his damndest every second of every day to make her change her mind.

"Carson!" she shouted.

"What!" he shouted back.

"Would you please just shut up and kiss me?"

Epilogue

They decided on a morning wedding, as Kate Beckett tended to wilt early. Kit asked timidly if they could have it in the garden, and Kate clapped her hands in delight. The women collaborated on the guest list. Margaret hired the tables and handwrote the invitations. Carson's Aunt Becky took care of the minister, the music and the food. It was a rushed affair, but everyone who knew them understood. Those who didn't were simply not invited.

Kit's cousin Liza, who was expecting a baby any day, sat by with her feet elevated while she filled Kit in with details of the family she was about to become a part of. Kit spent most of her time in town, as Carson was working day and night, trying to catch up with a backlog of work down at headquarters. "You understand," said Liza, "I can't vouch for any of this, but if only half of it is true, then PawPaw, who died recently, was about one part financial genius and three parts scalawag." They laughed quietly, and then Liza said, "Tell me something, cous—how much do you know about our Chandler ancestors?"

Kit shook her head. She was snapping beans into a bowl in her lap. None of the Becketts appeared in any big hurry, but none was allowed to sit idle, either, except for Liza, who was busy gestating. It was as if the entire family functioned as one big unit. She rather liked the feeling, although it took some getting used to.

"Well, let me tell you, our grandmother—no, she was our great-grandmother—she was a real pistol. They say she was almost as big as her husband, and could ride and shoot circles around any man on the ranch."

"Shoot circles?"

"Figure of speech." Liza laughed. "Hey, humor me, will you? Hormones gone haywire."

"Come on inside, ladies, it's lemonade time," someone called out.

And so it went. Kit had been absorbed into the family from the very first. Carson's mother, who was a dear and didn't seem as if she were suffering from anything more than slight confusion, insisted on showing her all the scrapbooks she'd filled...and then showing her again and again. She called her Emaline, and sometimes Abigail, but that was all right. Kit knew plenty of women with large families who had to call the roll before they hit on the right name.

Liza's husband, Lance, who was a pirate chaser, of all things, had called her Kit Carson and told her how, on some of the smaller islands along the coast, where only a few family names prevailed, wives were called by their own and their husband's given names, to avoid confusion.

They were about to go inside for lemonade when Carson arrived, walking silently up behind her on the lush grass to slide his arms down around her shoulders. "Miss me?" he whispered in her ear.

"I've been hearing stories."

"Uh-oh, I was afraid of that. Hi, Liza. Is the Buckett going to make it to the wedding?"

"He'll be in tonight. I told him he's not going to leave again until after my coming-out party, so if you want company on your honeymoon…"

"No thanks."

Carson's father met them at the back door, holding his wife's hand. Kate brightened when she saw her son, and greeted him by saying, "I can't recall your name at the moment, but the Lady Baltimore cake is on the sideboard." She frowned and her beloved Lancelot, third in a long line of Lancelots, led her back inside.

"Your folks will be in late tonight," Carson told Kit. "They'll be staying with Aunt Becky and Uncle Coley."

Kit rolled her eyes, and he laughed. "Hey, don't sweat it. Aunt Becky'll charm the socks off old Cast Iron, you just wait and see."

"No thanks. I plan to be busy, starting at eleven tomorrow morning." They'd scheduled the ceremony for eleven, with lunch in the garden to follow. After that, Carson and his bride would slip away to his cottage—more of a fishing retreat, really—on Kiawah Island.

"Ready to go home?" he asked her now.

Kit wanted to say she was already home, because she was. Carson's Aunt Becky had admired her earrings. His father had asked her if she followed baseball, and as it happened, she'd known the names of a few Braves players. He'd immediately declared her to be just the daughter he'd been waiting for.

Even Margaret had accepted her. "Lord, better you than me, honey. Have you seen that house of Car's?"

She'd laughed and added, "Well, of course you have, you two have been practically quarantined there ever since Car brought you home with him. Make him add a touch of color in the white paint, will you? Dead white is just so...you know. It lacks subtlety."

Margaret didn't. Lack subtlety, that was. She made no bones about being relieved that she was now free to go as far as her own ambition and talent would take her. Kit, for one, would be there to cheer her on.

"Tomorrow," Carson whispered as he led her away some half hour later, pausing to speak to friends, neighbors and family as they set up the chairs and tables and pruned his mother's flower garden. It was a promise, and Kit nodded, curling her hand into his warm, hard palm.

Tomorrow, and all the tomorrows to come.

*   *   *   *   *

Silhouette® Desire®

Bestselling author

Meagan McKinney

brings you three brand-new stories in
her engaging miniseries centered around
the town of Mystery, Montana, in

MATCHED IN MONTANA

*Wedding bells always ring
when the town matriarch plays Cupid!*

Coming in February 2003:
PLAIN JANE & THE HOTSHOT, SD #1493

Coming in March 2003:
THE COWBOY CLAIMS HIS LADY, SD #1499

Coming in April 2003:
BILLIONAIRE BOSS, SD #1505

Available at your favorite retail outlet.

Silhouette®

Where love comes alive™

COMING NEXT MONTH

#1489 SLEEPING BEAUTY'S BILLIONAIRE—Caroline Cross
Dynasties: The Barones
Years ago, Colleen Barone's mother had pressured her into breaking up with Gavin O'Sullivan. Then Colleen saw her gorgeous former flame at a wedding, and realized the old chemistry was still there. But the world-famous hotel magnate seemed to think she only wanted him now that he was rich. Somehow, Colleen had to convince Gavin she truly loved him—mind, body and soul!

#1490 KISS ME, COWBOY!—Maureen Child
After a bitter divorce, the last thing sexy single dad Mike Fallon wanted was to get romantically involved again. But when feisty Nora Bailey seemed determined to lose her virginity—with the town Casanova, no less—Mike rushed to her rescue. He soon found himself drowning in Nora's baby blues, but she wanted a husband. And he wasn't husband material…or was he?

#1491 THAT BLACKHAWK BRIDE—Barbara McCauley
Secrets!
Three days before her wedding, debutante Clair Beauchamp learned from handsome investigator Jacob Carver that she was really a Blackhawk from Texas. Realizing her whole life, including her almost-marriage, was a lie, Clair asked Jacob to reunite her with her family. But the impromptu road trip led to the consummation of their passionate attraction, and soon Clair yearned to make their partnership permanent.

#1492 CHARMING THE PRINCE—Laura Wright
Time was running out; if Prince Maxim Thorne didn't find a bride, his father would find one for him. So Max set out to seduce the lovely Francesca Charming, certain his father would never agree to his marrying a commoner and would thus drop his marriage demand. But what started out as make-believe turned into undeniable passion…. Might marrying Francesca give Max the fairy-tale ending he hadn't known he wanted?

#1493 PLAIN JANE & THE HOTSHOT—Megan McKinney
Matched in Montana
Shy Joanna Lofton met charismatic smoke-jumping firefighter Nick Kramer while on a mountain retreat. Joanna worried she wasn't exciting enough for a man like Nick, but her fears proved unfounded, for the fires raging around them couldn't compare to the flame of attraction burning between them.

#1494 AT THE TYCOON'S COMMAND—Shawna Delacorte
When Kim Donaldson inherited a debt to Jared Stevens's family, she agreed to work as Jared's assistant for the summer. Despite a generations-old family feud, as Kim and Jared worked together, their relationship took a decidedly romantic turn. But could they put the past behind them before it tore them apart?